THE BEACHFRONT CHRISTMAS...

AINSLEY KEATON

CHAPTER 1

SAMANTHA

*S*amantha Flynn, Ava's daughter, was still on Nantucket but that would soon change. Her boyfriend Grayson had been working on a fantasy novel for the better part of three years. It was a doorstopper of a book, and he self-published it. He told Samantha that plenty of fantasy authors were self-publishing their books and making major money on them.

Grayson sent his book to a whole crew of beta readers, and beta readers were all unanimous about the book - Grayson wrote a winner. Beta readers were people who read and review books before they were published. These readers were telling him that it was very good.

And then Grayson published the book, ran a bunch of ads for it, and hit the market just right. He got really lucky and somehow, the book ended up on the Kindle belonging to Cecelia Knox, a Netflix executive and was very interested in creating a limited series out of the book. Apparently, Cecelia was sick one weekend and had nothing to do but read. She came across Grayson's book that weekend and loved it.

It was a lucky break, for sure. The upshot was that

Grayson wanted to move to Los Angeles to be closer to the action. He had meetings lined up with various Netflix executives, and, hopefully, this book would be picked up for a limited-run series. If it was, Grayson imagined he would be involved in many more meetings. So, Grayson decided that he and Samantha should move to Los Angeles.

At first, Samantha didn't like the idea. She'd made a name for herself there on Nantucket as the creator of beautiful, creative, and original cakes of all types. She really enjoyed making wedding cakes, but she soon found herself making cakes for other occasions as well. Anniversaries, birthdays, gender reveals, wedding and baby showers – Samantha cheerfully made cakes for all these occasions and more. She was getting very good at it, and she was very much in demand. Javier, her boss and the man who owned the bakery where she worked, loved her work and had given her several raises, promotions and bonuses because he wanted to keep her happy.

And she *was* happy at the bakery. Very happy. She felt that if she left Javier, she would be doing him dirty. He had been hinting around to her about making her a partner in the bakery, which would really increase her yearly salary.

But Grayson was adamant that he wanted to move to Los Angeles. He pretty much told Samantha he was going to move to the West Coast whether she came or not. This left her with no choice but to say yes to him. There was just no way that Samantha was going to let her best friend and boyfriend, Grayson, live across the country from her. So, she agreed to move with him.

Some headhunters from Los Angeles had contacted Samantha, so she called back the headhunters and agreed to come out to Los Angeles for the best job they could find for her, and that was how she got a new job with one of the top wedding bakeries and catering firms in Los Angeles, called the Sweet Fantasy Bakery. This was a bakery that often catered to celebrity events, so Samantha was very much looking forward to meeting some television and movie actors, actresses, and directors. Maybe even meet a reality star or two.

In the meantime, it was time to pack, and that thought overwhelmed her. Oh, she hated moving. But the thing of it was, the place where she and Grayson were currently staying was tiny. It was basically the mother-in-law quarters of a gay couple. It was designed just like the large house but was about 1/3 of the size of the large house. Because of that, she and Grayson didn't accumulate too much over the years.

Nevertheless, she looked around her house and despaired. There was a part of her that was desperate for some kind of stability in her life. Her life before coming to Nantucket was so unstable that Samantha often feared dying quite young. She always took a lot of chances in her life, chances that were not exactly advisable. Whether she was meeting a random guy across the country after only talking to him on the Internet, or walking home from the bar at 3 o'clock in the morning through sketchy neighborhoods, Samantha lived life on the edge. And she was so ready to change it that she was thrilled to be living on tiny little Nantucket, where she didn't think she could get into much trouble.

Of course, Samantha being Samantha, she did get into trouble when she first got to Nantucket. She almost drowned in the ocean and was saved by a dude named Adrian, who was wealthy and a bit of a douche. No, he wasn't a bit of a douche, but a full-on one. Samantha was over him from the first date, and then she dated another rich guy, and finally ended up with Grayson, her best friend of six years who had loved her all along.

And the stability of the tiny island was a great relief for

Samantha. She no longer had to worry about walking through sketchy neighborhoods and looking over her shoulder for some bad guy to pop out and attack her. Because she found love with Grayson, she wasn't looking for randos on the internet anymore. In short, Samantha no longer feared she would be dead by the age of 30.

Now, she was moving to another big city, and she wondered if it was going to be a step backward for her. She worried she would fall back into some of her old bad habits when she moved out to Los Angeles.

But she was excited about being out there because she wanted to be closer to her family. Both her mother and her aunt were living out there, and Samantha had just gotten to know her Aunt Sarah and she really loved her. And now her mother and her Aunt Sarah were opening up a winery together, and it would be perfect if Samantha's new bakery, the Sweet Fantasy bakery, could partner with Sarah's new winery.

After all, the Sweet Fantasy bakery not only supplied wedding cakes for different functions but also catered events. These events, of course, needed lots and lots of alcohol, especially wine. So Sarah talked to the bakery about the possibility they would supply cakes to functions held at the winery, and they would use wines from the winery for the other functions the bakery catered to.

Her new boss, Kayla Brentwood, seemed to love Samantha. The two had exchanged emails and had spoken to one another on Zoom several times. And they seemed to really click with one another. Their personalities meshed really well. Kayla wasn't too much older than Samantha - she was only 30 years old, and Samantha had just turned 25. Samantha was very bubbly and very unfiltered in her speech, so she and Kayla chatted over Zoom about everything under the sun. They talked about movies they'd seen, series they loved, reality shows they were digging, and music.

It was ostensibly a job interview, but Samantha forgot that the purpose of the Zoom call was that Kayla was looking to hire a new cake decorator. She started to feel like she was chatting with a brand-new friend. By the time the Zoom call was through, about an hour after it began, Kayla formally offered Samantha the job with the Sweet Fantasy Bakery, and Samantha gleefully accepted.

Then it was a matter of talking to Javier, who didn't take the news well. "Samantha, you can't do this," he pleaded. "It's summertime. This is my biggest time of year. I have weddings lined up all summer long, and I need you." He looked like he wanted to cry. Samantha felt badly for him but at the same time, she couldn't arrange her entire life around him.

"I'm really sorry. But, like I said, Grayson's moving to Los Angeles, and I'm going with him. I'm sorry. Really I am, but I have no choice."

Javier shook his head. "I made you. If it weren't for me, you would be nobody. This is how you repay me?"

Samantha took a deep breath. Javier was not at all being fair. After all, the only reason why Samantha got the gig that made her, which was a society wedding for which she absolutely nailed the cake, was because the previous cake maker had quit with no notice at all. And, at first, Javier did not want Samantha to work on that cake. In fact, he made phone calls all that day trying to find somebody, anybody, who would be able to do it on short notice. Samantha stepped up to the plate and saved Javier's bacon, but it wasn't Javier's choice at all. In fact, if it was up to Javier, the previous baker, whose name was Cynthia, would still be making the wedding cakes for the bakery. Javier just wasn't going to give

Samantha a chance to do anything creative if not for the fact that the emergency forced his hand.

"Javier, again, I'm sorry," Samantha said. "But I seem to remember you making phone calls to everybody and their brother and sister when Cynthia quit that day because you didn't want me to work on that cake at all. So, maybe you made me, but it wasn't your choice. It was Cynthia who irresponsibly left you without any notice at all. I'm giving you two weeks' notice, unlike her. Now, there's nothing you can do to change my mind about leaving for Los Angeles. So I suggest you don't even try."

Samantha wasn't usually so stern with her words, but Javier really pissed her off. He was trying to guilt trip her into staying, and that really made Samantha see red. If there is one thing she hated, it was a manipulative person. And that's exactly what Javier was trying to do. Manipulate her.

Javier knew he was in the wrong because he knew what Samantha was saying was right. He didn't want her to work the Lawrence wedding. He even referred to her as an amateur. Now, he needed her, and he was going to make life difficult for her by making her feel guilty. Samantha wasn't going to be having that.

Javier shook his head and started talking rapidly in Spanish. Samantha didn't know a word of Spanish, so she had no idea what he was saying but she was sure she heard at least a few Spanish curse words.

"Okay, just go, go. You don't even have to give me two weeks' notice. In fact, I don't want to see your face anymore, so go."

Samantha just rolled her eyes. Talk about cutting off your nose to spite your face, she thought. There was a wedding that was coming up that weekend, and Samantha had planned to make the cake for that wedding. But, since Javier was essentially firing by telling her she couldn't put in notice, he was going to have to find somebody on short notice again. Instead of doing things professionally by allowing Samantha to put in notice and make the cake for that wedding, he was letting his temper get the best of him. And he was going to pay for it because Samantha was going to take him up on his offer to just leave.

After all, Grayson was already out in Los Angeles, waiting for her to move out there as well. Grayson had a bunch of meetings set up, so he couldn't wait around for her to get out from under her job. He had to get out there, stat. He needed to strike while the iron was hot, which was what he was doing. So, Grayson was out in Los Angeles and Samantha was stuck on Nantucket because she wanted to do the responsible thing and give notice to the bakery before quitting.

Now, Javier was freeing her from her obligation to be responsible and professional. So, Samantha was going to fly out to Los Angeles that evening. Grayson had already found an apartment out in LA, and he had already gotten furniture out there as well. All Samantha had to do was pack her personal things, which weren't a lot because Grayson took most of Samantha's things when he moved out to Los Angeles, and fly.

"Okay," Samantha said. "I guess you're just going to have to find somebody else to make the cake for this weekend's wedding. Good luck with that."

Javier just disgustedly waved a hand at her and scowled. "Go," he ordered.

"Going, going," Samantha said.

Then she went home, packed, and booked a flight to Los Angeles.

Grayson was going to be so surprised and thrilled.

CHAPTER 2

SARAH

*S*arah was absolutely giddy. She'd hired somebody
to make sure the tasting room was up and running,
and the grapes were almost ready to harvest. She had also
managed to get a liquor license, so the winery was ready to
open. The previous winery owner had already manufactured
a great line of wines in the enormous stainless steel tanks in
the cellar. So, even though Sarah planned to create wines her
way when she harvested the grapes, at the moment, she was
going to offer the wine that she had inherited from the
previous owner of the winery.

So now it was time to promote the winery. The first thing
she did was contact Kayla Brentwood, who was her niece,
Samantha's new boss. Kayla was the owner of a very
successful bakery there in town, which also had a catering
arm that was just as successful. Kayla was quite young, so
Sarah didn't quite know why she was such a success. Then
she found out that the Sweet Fantasy Bakery originally was
started by Kayla's parents who recently died in a car acci-
dent, and Kayla took over.

However it was that Kayla got her gig with the bakery

was of no concern to Sarah. What mattered was that Kayla was looking for a new venue to hold some of her events, and she was also looking for a new winery to supply her wines. Since Kayla was fairly new to running the business, even though she'd worked for the bakery and catering since she was only 10 years old, she was looking for new blood to partner with. Samantha had found Sarah when she found out Kayla was looking for somebody to partner with, and she urged her to contact Kayla immediately.

So, Sarah gave Kayla a call, and the two women agreed to meet for coffee later that day. And then Sarah called Mary, who was her stepdaughter, Julia's, aunt. Mary was watching Julia while Sarah was working. Although Sarah and Quinn had agreed to watch one another's children when they could, as, hopefully, when the winery got going Sarah would be working evenings while Quinn worked days, Sarah would be working day and night until the winery opened officially.

Ava was Sarah's partner in the winery business, and she, too, would be working around the clock until things were ready to go. At the moment, Ava wasn't around because she had an emergency at her home because her pipes had burst for some reason. But she would be coming to the winery later that day.

Mary sounded strange on the phone when Sarah called her. "Sarah," she said. "I'm so glad you called. I think you better get home. Something is blowing up and I need to talk to you about it."

Sarah just scrunched her eyebrows. What was Mary talking about? "What's going on?"

Mary seemed to take a deep breath on the other side of the line. "It's Julia. My sister Hannah has filed a lawsuit."

"What kind of a lawsuit?"

"A custody lawsuit. She wants custody of Julia."

CHAPTER 3

SAMANTHA

*S*amantha got to Los Angeles, and the first thing she did was announce her arrival to Grayson, who was in their new apartment, working hard on the follow-up to his first fantasy novel. He had several meetings with some Netflix executives later on in the day, so he only had a few minutes to give Samantha a kiss on the lips and help her unpack.

"I'm so glad you're here," he said eagerly. "I really missed you."

Samantha missed Grayson, too. The two best friends had not spent too many days apart since they met all those years ago. And they really hadn't spend much time apart since they officially became a couple.

"Me too. Anyhow, what's going on with you right now?" Samantha asked.

"I told you, I have some meetings with some Netflix people at 2 o'clock. What are you doing?"

"Well, I'm going to my new bakery. I just called Kayla and told her that I would be free early, and she wants me to come on in. She's really anxious for me to start baking cakes and so forth. And then, after I go to the bakery and she shows me around a bit, I'm going to my mom's winery."

Samantha flopped down on the couch. " I can't believe I'm here. I'm sorry, this whole thing just has been such a whirlwind. It seems like I've lived a million lives just in the past year or so. And now it seems I'm going to live a million more lives."

Grayson sat next to her and smiled. "Here's the thing, Samantha. No matter how many lives you've lived, you've lived them and you've come out on top. And you're going to do great here, too. Just think, you're going to be catering events and making cakes for parties where celebrities are going to be. Honest to God celebrities. Who knows, you might meet Chris Hemsworth."

Samantha started to giggle. Samantha and Grayson both agreed that Chris Hemsworth would be Samantha's hall pass. "That would be amazing, but I'd take his brother Liam, too."

"I'll bet you will," Grayson said. "Anyhow, I think you're going to love it out here. I predict you're going to fit right in. You've always seemed like a California girl to me, anyhow, with your blonde hair and your bubbly personality. I think you've finally found your home."

Samantha looked at Grayson. "Grayson, please say this is my home. And that you and I will start looking for a place to buy. Maybe a condo or something like that. I really don't want to do another move."

Samantha didn't say as much, but she was thinking that every move she made - from Brooklyn to Nantucket and then from Nantucket to Los Angeles – was because Grayson wanted those moves. When Grayson moved to Nantucket, Samantha had no idea what he was thinking. He told Samantha that he wanted to live by a beach, but she had no idea exactly why Nantucket came to mind. So she ended up moving from Brooklyn to Nantucket to be close to him, even though they were just really good friends at that time. And now, with the move to Los Angeles, he had an actual reason for being out here. It was going to be good for Grayson's new career for him to be in Los Angeles, and Samantha couldn't argue with that.

Samantha was following Grayson around, and she was tired of moving. Next thing you know, Grayson might tell her that he wanted to go to Europe for some odd reason, and he would expect Samantha to follow him out there, too. Samantha wanted to put her foot down, and she wanted to put down roots, too. And the best way to do that, Samantha thought, was for the two of them to actually buy a place to live.

The ideal would be a house, just in case the two of them decided one day to have a family, and, even if they didn't have a family, they might want a dog. And Samantha always had a hard time picturing a dog in a high-rise, just because it would be such a pain taking the pooch down the long elevator ride every time it had to use the bathroom. She much would rather be able to just open up the door and let the pooch out in the backyard. But Samantha also knew that most houses were way beyond their means, at least for the moment.

Then again, if Grayson's Netflix show actually materialized for real and became a hit, the two of them could afford a house. But Samantha knew the Grayson Netflix thing was in the early stages, and anything could happen. Maybe nothing would happen.

He was doing very well with book sales, however, so he was making pretty good money on Amazon with his book. Not enough to buy a house, but enough to pay the bills every month and then some. And Samantha was going to make pretty good money, not six figures or anything like that, but enough that the two of them could live comfortably in their apartment, assuming that Grayson's sales didn't crash to the floor, which was a concern.

Samantha knew that with the self-publishing game, it was a matter of feeding the beast with new books all the time, or else you start sinking down the ranks. She understood there was something like a 30-day cliff or maybe it was 60 days, where the book becomes less visible and falls precipitously down the ranks. And once it fell precipitously down the ranks, sales plummet and so does income. The way she knew all this was because Grayson himself told her about it. He did his research on Amazon and how their rankings went, and that was what he understood about it. So, if nothing happened with the Netflix thing, Grayson would be relying on a very volatile income source. There was a possibility they'd soon be living on Samantha's income, which wouldn't be enough for the two of them to live as comfortably as they were now.

So, the sad thing was, Samantha still didn't feel she was on solid ground. She wondered if she would ever feel the sense of income security that her mother felt when working for the big law firm.

Then again, she was doing something that she absolutely loved, and that was worth its weight in gold. She knew most people her age couldn't say the same – they were working at jobs they didn't like and didn't fulfill them, working for unreasonable bosses and working with coworkers who stole their lunch. She was being fulfilled creatively, and it seemed that Kayla would be a great boss. It seemed it was a good trade-off, in the end, to work a job that she loved even if it wasn't the most high-paying.

If only the cost of living wasn't so high in Los Angeles, Samantha would be much happier.

Grayson kissed her on the lips, and she sighed. Once they finally decided they were going to be a couple, or, to be exact, she was the one who decided they'd be a couple, because he always wanted to be a couple but he never told her that, Samantha was finally fulfilled on the romantic front as well. She was always amazed just how well they got along in bed. Somehow, during all those years she knew him as only her best friend and surrogate big brother, she never imagined him to be quite the lover he was.

"Samantha, this is your home. Los Angeles is going to be where we're going to buy a house one day with a porch swing and a backyard for all the fur babies you're going to want and maybe a rugrat or two. And we're going to swing on the porch swing together when we're 90 years old. I hope that answers your question."

"Oh, it does. It does."

Samantha hoped that Grayson wasn't just telling her pretty words.

Because the scenario he laid out for her made her smile.

CHAPTER 4

SARAH

Sarah called Ava and told her she had an emergency. She wanted Ava to go ahead and meet with Kayla, as the meeting with Kayla was just too important to blow off.

At the same time, there was just no way that Sarah was going to let Julia's Aunt Hannah get the upper hand in any way, shape, or form. She was going to slap her down and put her in her place as soon as possible.

At least, she hoped she would.

" Sure," Ava said when Sarah called her to explain the situation. "I'll be more than happy to meet with Kayla. I'd like to meet her anyway since she's going to be my daughter's boss."

Sarah just nodded as she drove down the mountainous roads. She had such a creeping sense of panic in her chest. In the back of her mind, she knew this could happen. After all, her link to Julia was tenuous at best. It was made somewhat stronger by the fact that she was married to Julia's father Max, however briefly. But that didn't mean she was automatically assumed to be Julia's guardian.

She'd hoped that nothing like this would happen, though.

After all, Mary didn't have the financial means to take care of Julia. And Mary didn't seem interested in doing that, anyhow. However, Mary was a wonderful aunt to Julia and watched her whenever Sarah needed her to.

Julia and Mary got along extremely well. Sarah didn't know it until recently, but Julia was very artistic like Mary. Sarah found this out one day when she went to pick up Julia after Mary watched her, and Mary said that the two of them had been painting landscapes. Mary proudly showed Julia's painting, and Sarah was astounded. The young girl had a lot of promising talent for painting.

Besides both of them being very artistic, they also both loved the water and they both were excellent surfers. So, the upshot was that Julia really enjoyed visiting Mary, and Mary, who admitted to Sarah that she was quite lonely, really enjoyed Julia's company as well. She said she and Julia got along famously, and Sarah saw that for herself. The bond between Julia and Mary was very tight. Sarah saw that their personalities just meshed well. They had similar senses of humor, they were interested in similar things, and they even liked the same movies.

But Mary couldn't take custody of Julia because she didn't have the money for it. Sarah understood that, as did Julia. That was the reason why the arrangement was as it was – Julia would live with Sarah, Quinn and Emerson, but, since they lived so close to one another, Mary would watch Julia and Emerson as often as she could. Since Mary worked from home as an artist, she was very flexible with her hours, which helped.

So far, it was working extremely well. It was still the middle of summer, so Sarah knew that things might become a bit more complicated when school started for the girls, especially for Emerson, who was going to a high school for the arts that was about a half-hour away from their Venice

Beach home. Julia was going to go to the local high school, so getting her to and from the school was going to be less of a hassle than for Emerson. Nevertheless, Sarah knew she could handle the logistics of Julia going to school when the time came.

She was so confident that she was going to do a good job raising the girl. She was excited about it. She had a regret that she wasn't able to bring up a child from birth and guide that child through life. But she was going to get a chance to at least mentor Julia. She was hopeful she could really become a true mother to the girl.

Now, this. Apparently Hannah, the aunt Julia didn't get along with, felt she should have custody of Julia. Hannah didn't even go to Max's funeral. It wasn't like she didn't know her brother was dead – Mary told Sarah she'd called Hannah several times about it and spoken with her. Hannah simply said she was busy and she sent a card. She didn't even bother to send flowers, only a card.

And now, here she was, believing she was the one who was going to raise Julia. And Sarah thought that that was the worst possible scenario for the young girl.

Max was going to make sure that Sarah was the one who raised Julia by filing some legal paperwork to make Sarah Julia's legal guardian. That, combined with the fact that Sarah and Max were legally married at the time of his death, would've been enough for any court to declare that Sarah was Julia's guardian. However, he died before he was able to get this paperwork in place. Which meant Sarah was vulnerable. Sarah really had no legal right to Julia, even though she was married to Max. Perhaps a judge might take Sarah's short-lived marriage to Max into consideration when a custody battle got going, but Sarah knew Hannah probably had a superior claim.

Sarah finally got to Mary's house. Julia immediately saw

her pull up, and she ran out to her car. The young girl had been crying. Mary also came out to the car, and Sarah saw somebody she didn't know standing on the porch. The woman was around 60 years old, with graying hair, a perfectly straight posture, and a frown on her face. She resembled Mary in a very superficial way, in that they both had the same kinds of features and body type. Like Mary, this woman was tall, around 5'9", and quite thin. They had the same blue eyes, the same straight nose, and the same bow-shaped lips.

While the resemblance to Mary was superficial, the vibe Sarah got from this woman was much different from Mary's. While Mary was laid-back and a free spirit - she was a woman who painted her fingernails bright green and her toenails bright purple when she wasn't painting each finger-nail a different color, and she was also a woman who dyed her graying hair with streaks of pink - this woman obviously was the opposite. Even though it was June, and it was extremely hot out, she was wearing a pantsuit. Her graying hair was tied back in a severe bun, and her fingernails were painted with a neutral shade of beige.

Sarah didn't need to be told who this was. This was obviously the infamous aunt Hannah.

Sarah swallowed hard. She had her arm around Julia as she walked to the porch. "Hello," Sarah said. "I'm Sarah. Julia's stepmom."

The woman just nodded slightly. "Hannah. Very nice to meet you."

While Hannah said it was very nice to meet Sarah, the look on her face said anything but. It was obvious she held Sarah in disdain, even before Sarah said a single word. Hannah looked at Sarah up and down, obviously not approving of Sarah's typical uniform, which consisted of jean shorts, a tank top, and a jean jacket. Sarah typically wore some kind of sandal every day. She hadn't put on a pair of socks since she came to California.

Could Sarah really blame Hannah for holding her in disdain? After all, Sarah was, for all intents and purposes, a rando. She barely knew Max at the time he died, she wasn't Jewish, and she knew so little about the family that she didn't even really recognize Hannah when she saw her. She really wasn't privy to the family dynamics of the Stein family. She knew Mary, and she was becoming close friends with her. And, of course, she knew Julia, although she could stand to know her stepdaughter a bit better.

Nevertheless, Julia had chosen to live with Sarah. That had to count for something, didn't it? She was going to have to talk to Ava about the situation as soon as possible. Even though Ava was a tax attorney in her old job in New York City, she still had a passing knowledge of different kinds of law, including domestic law. So, hopefully, Ava could give her a bit of advice about the situation. And, of course, Sarah would have to find an attorney who specialized in family law.

"Aunt Sarah," Julia said as she sobbed in Sarah's arms. "Hannah wants me to go back to New York City with her to live. I don't want to go with her."

Julia said this to Sarah loud enough for Hannah to hear her. But, as Sarah looked at Hannah's face, Sarah realized Hannah probably didn't care that Julia was sobbing about not wanting to go with her. Hannah just narrowed her eyes and shook her head as Julia sobbed in Sarah's arms.

Mary was standing to the side, watching the scene between Julia and Sarah with a frown on her face. And then she looked over at Hannah. "Do you see what you're doing? Take a look at that girl and tell me you think you're doing what's best for her."

Hannah raised an eyebrow. "I need to talk to Sarah alone."

19

When Hannah said that, Julia wrapped her arms even tighter around Sarah's waist. "Don't leave me, Aunt Sarah."

"Honey, I need to talk to your Aunt Hannah," Sarah said. "Maybe I can talk to her and make her see that taking you away to New York City is wrong. But I do have to talk to her because if I just try to ignore her, it's just going to make everything worse."

Mary came over to Julia and gently pried her away from Sarah. "Dear, I think we need to leave Aunt Hannah and Sarah alone to talk."

Sarah took a deep breath as Mary and Julia walked back into Mary's house. She just stood and looked at the ramrod straight-backed Hannah. "Okay," Sarah said. "Go ahead, let's talk."

Hannah once again nodded slightly at her. "Join me on the porch?"

Hannah climbed the porch and sat on one of the chairs that were around a small table. Sarah went over to the porch swing and sat down. Sarah tucked one of her legs under her rear end and put her hand on the chain that held up the swing.

Sarah could see on Hannah's face that she disapproved of Sarah and how casual she was. But Sarah didn't care. She was who she was. Maybe she was trying to be even more casual than usual because she wanted to demonstrate to Hannah that she wasn't to be intimidated. Or, maybe not. She didn't really know her own motivation for being so outwardly laid-back about the entire thing. Maybe it was because inside, her gut was roiling and she felt a bit nauseated. So she deliberately wanted to look calmer on the outside than she really was.

Sarah just stared at Hannah for a little while, willing Hannah to make the first move. The last thing she wanted to do was to make the first move herself because she felt that if she did, she'd be put at a disadvantage in the conversation.

Hannah just sat on the chair, her back still perfectly straight, her head held very high. Sarah wondered if Hannah's posture was always so ramrod straight, or if Hannah was trying to intimidate Sarah the way Sarah was trying to intimidate Hannah. Sarah was trying to intimidate Hannah by affecting body language that made her look like she just didn't care. Hannah was trying to intimidate Sarah by affecting body language which looked like she was ready to go to war.

Sarah also wondered if Hannah was dying of heatstroke at the moment. It was almost 100 degrees out, and she was wearing a damn pantsuit. With hose and pumps. Sarah felt hot just looking at the woman.

Finally, after what seemed like hours but probably were only minutes, Hannah cleared her throat. "Julia refers to you as Aunt Sarah. Why is that?"

Sarah sighed. "It's because I'm close with her actual aunt and I was married to her father, so she uses the term 'Aunt Sarah' as a term of endearment."

What an odd question, Sarah thought. Calling a woman aunt this or aunt was a perfectly acceptable term of endearment even if the woman technically was not a blood relation to the child calling her "aunt." For instance, Sarah had a good friend when she was living in Los Angeles and was working for the architectural firm that was her first job out of college. This friend had a daughter who always called Sarah "Aunt Sarah." What was the big deal about that?

Hannah raised an eyebrow. "But you're supposed to be her guardian."

Sarah rolled her eyes, even though she tried not to show Hannah any contempt. But she couldn't help it. Hannah was keeping her so off balance that she had to let off a little steam.

"Yes, you're right," Sarah said. "I guess I can ask Julia to call me Guardian Sarah or Stepmother Sarah, but that would all sound pretty silly."

"Why don't you ask her to just call you Sarah?"

"Because she chooses to call me Aunt Sarah, that's why. Why are you being so weird about this?" Sarah asked.

Sarah crossed her arms as she realized this woman was getting under her last nerve. She took a deep breath and tried to tell herself not to let Hannah get under her skin. But, Sarah was only human, and this woman was threatening her stepdaughter's happiness. Sarah was surprised at how much like a mama grizzly she was starting to feel. Maybe Julia was only her stepdaughter, and maybe she was only Julia's guardian, not her mother, but she felt very protective towards the girl.

Hannah merely grimaced when Sarah asked her why she was being so weird about Julia referring to Sarah as "Aunt" Sarah. "I was just wondering, is all. There's no need for you to be defensive."

"Are you planning on filing a custody case?" Sarah asked Hannah. No need to beat around the bush.

"I am. I wanted to see if you would accept service, so I didn't have to hire a process server. If you will, I have a form for you to fill out. You'll have to have it notarized, of course."

Sara knitted her eyebrows. God, this woman was weird. She had a curiously flat affect. As if she just didn't care that she was wrecking everybody's life. And, indeed, she probably didn't care. That would be the reason why Julia didn't get along with her. This woman seemed to not have a compassionate or empathetic bone in her body.

"No. I'm not going to sign any form of yours. I'm sorry,

22

but I don't know why you think I want to make this easy on you."

" Okay," Hannah said. "I guess that's all that needs to be said. I'll go ahead and get my process server to formally serve you. I know you're part owner of a winery, and you're going to be having some functions sometime soon. I think I'll have the process server show up in the middle of one of your parties that you plan on throwing in your new winery."

Sarah felt her hackles rising. What did this woman think she was doing? Hannah seemed to be on a war footing, and perhaps Sarah was just being caught unaware of this fact. At any rate, she was certainly caught flat-footed by it all.

"Give me the form to sign. I'll take it to a notary and sign it."

Hannah nodded. "I brought one. He's waiting in my SUV. Just a second."

Sarah impatiently tapped her fingers on the side of the porch swing as Hannah went to her SUV, opened the door, and brought out an embarrassed-looking man who was around 50 years old. The man and Hannah came up to the porch, and the man produced a document out of his satchel and placed it on the porch table.

Sarah reluctantly went over to the porch table as she read over the document stating she accepted service of the custody petition. She signed the document, the man notarized it, and Hannah handed over the petition for Sarah to look over.

After the guy finished notarizing the document, Hannah dismissively waved her hand at him and pointed to the SUV. The guy nodded his head and walked back to the car and got in.

Sarah rapidly read over the petition. The petition didn't state any specific grounds for why Hannah wanted custody of Julia. The petition simply stated that Sarah was neither blood relation nor declared the legal guardian for Julia. It also stated that Hannah was Julia's closest living relative, therefore should presumptively be declared the proper guardian for Julia. There was also something written into the petition that Sarah was not Jewish, and that Judaism was important to Julia. Other than that, it was difficult to understand on what grounds Hannah was seeking custody. There was certainly not an allegation of abuse or neglect, which Sarah was aware were the main grounds for changing custody in a situation like this.

"Why are you doing this?" Sarah asked Hannah.

"Because I'm Julia's aunt. I'm her blood relation. You're nobody to her."

The words stung Sarah. She wasn't prepared for the woman to be so blunt in her words. She didn't really know why she wasn't prepared for this, but she wasn't. She supposed that Hannah's words hurt so much because Sarah knew they were true. Sarah wasn't anybody to Julia. She barely knew the young girl, and she barely knew the young girl's father, even though she was married to him.

"You say I'm nobody to her. But I am somebody to her. I'm her stepmother."

Hannah snorted and her posture got even straighter, as if that was a possibility. "Stepmother? You're calling yourself her stepmother? You married my brother while he was drunk. You took advantage of his inebriated state. And you weren't married to him that long. I don't know exactly why you think that you have custodial rights to my niece when you barely know her and you hardly knew her dad. And you don't know her family, at all."

Hannah got the marriage scenario exactly backward, Sarah thought ruefully. *She* was the one who was out of her mind drunk, and *Max* was the one who took advantage of the situation. But, whatever...

"Listen-"

"And, you're a shiksa," she said in a tone of voice that left nothing to the imagination. "A blonde shiksa at that." Hannah then crossed her arms. Apparently, the color of Sarah's hair made her all the more undesirable in Hannah's eyes.

"So? What's that supposed to mean, I'm a blonde shiksa? Why does it matter what color my hair is?" Sarah was aware that there were plenty of blonde Jews in the world, so she was curious as to why Hannah seemed to find her hair color so intolerable.

Hannah simply raised an eyebrow. "It doesn't matter if you're blonde, brunette or sport pink hair like my crazy sister. What matters is that you're not one of us. So I don't see how you can possibly hope to bring Julia up properly."

Sarah decided to take a different tact with this woman. Perhaps she could catch more bees with honey than vinegar. That was what her mother always told her, ironically, because her mother was not known for sweet-talking anybody. Yet, Sarah thought that was, in general, good advice. Try to kiss somebody's ass instead of banging them over the head.

"Listen, Hannah," Sarah said. "I know what you're saying. It's true, I'm not Jewish. However, I've been studying Hebrew and I've been to several services with Julia. I've really enjoyed the services, and I plan on taking her every Saturday."

"Well, good for you. I'm so happy to know you've gone to what, two services now? Two entire services? Why you're practically ready to have a Bat Mitzvah."

Sarah didn't want to admit ignorance, so she didn't question Hannah when she sarcastically suggested that Sarah do her Bat Mitzvah. Sarah knew a little bit about Bat Mitzvahs. She knew they typically were given to young Jewish girls when they turn 13, and young Jewish boys were given Bar Mitzvahs at the same age. She had never been to one of these affairs, but she knew one of the prerequisites was that the child knew Hebrew.

What Sarah didn't know, and what she was too afraid to ask, was whether a Bat Mitzvah was appropriate for an adult. She'd never heard of an adult doing a Bat Mitzvah. She knew a little bit about what it took to convert to Judaism, mainly because she was a fan of *Sex and the City*, and Charlotte had converted to Judaism to marry Harry. Charlotte had to contact a Rabbi, and at some point, she did some kind of a bath to become reborn or something of the sort. Sarah wasn't exactly sure what any of that meant. And she certainly wasn't going to show her ignorance by asking Hannah about it.

"Well, maybe I will do a Bat Mitzvah. How about that? It's never too late to become a Jew."

Hannah snorted again. Sarah was really starting to become annoyed with Hannah's snorting. It was so dismissive. It just smacked of entitlement. It was as if Hannah knew she had the upper hand on the custody issue, and she was lording it over Sarah.

Indeed, Sarah thought that was probably the case. Hannah probably *did* think she was entitled to custody of Julia, and she was going to let Sarah know that was the case. Maybe Hannah had her doubts about what she was doing, but if that were the case, she was not letting on. She clearly thought she was superior to Sarah, and she was going to let Sarah know about it. In no uncertain terms.

"It's never too late to become a Jew? Do you hear yourself? What do you know about Judaism?"

"I know I love the music at the services," Sarah said. "And, like I said, I'm learning Hebrew so I can understand the services a bit better. And I'm willing to learn anything at all, just so I can become a better guardian for Julia. At any rate, my not being Jewish shouldn't be the only thing you're worried about here."

Hannah shook her head. "That's not the only thing I worry about, obviously. But it is a major thing. I understand that you were raised by an atheist."

"I was. So what?"

"So what? So what? Tell me a little bit about your religious leanings."

Sarah took a deep breath. She wasn't liking where this was going, to say the very least. "Well, I haven't really had any. When I was younger, I was interested in Buddhism. It seemed like a beautiful religion that was focused on non-materialism, which attracted me. And, for a little while, I was attending a Unitarian-Universalist church."

"Unitarian-Universalist," Hannah said with disgust. "That's not even a church at all. It's not even a religion."

"No. I agree, it's not really a religion, per se. It focuses on good works that all of us can perform in this life and social justice. So, I don't know, it seems much more like a religion than the place that preaches fire and brimstone and tells you that you have a path to salvation even if you hate your fellow man."

Sarah raised an eyebrow. She knew that she was getting away from the topic at hand, because Judaism wasn't a religion that preached fire and brimstone, and much of it was focused on charity and good works in this world. She had been disgusted with a lot of organized religions, that was true. But Judaism seemed like a faith she could really get behind. She loved that some of the central tenets of the faith were equality, social justice, and fairness. To Sarah, any religion that focused on these concepts was a religion she could embrace.

"So, you were interested in Buddhism when you were young, and you attended a few services at a church that wasn't really a church. Other than that, what do you even know about religion?"

"No much," Sarah said. "Which is a good thing, isn't it? I mean, after all, if I were dead set on being a, say, evangelical Christian or something of the sort, I wouldn't be willing to convert to Judaism. But, because I don't really have a religion I've followed, I'm pretty much a tabula rasa. That means I'm willing to be open-minded about the whole situation."

"That's a creative way of looking at it," Hannah said sarcastically. "You've spent your whole life avoiding religion, so you can just embrace any religion. Sorry, but I'm not buying it."

Sarah stood up. "Listen. As I said, this can't be the only reason why you're doing this to us. Religion can't be the only grounds that you're going to try to screw up Julia's life. Because if you take her to New York City, that's exactly what you're going to be doing. Screwing her up."

"And why, pray tell, do you say that my taking custody of my only niece is quote screwing her up? You don't know the first thing about her."

"Neither do you," Sarah said. "You didn't even bother to come to Max's funeral. What's that about?"

"I had a trial that week," Hannah said. "I know you don't understand anything about work responsibilities, so you couldn't possibly understand why I couldn't come to the West Coast for his funeral. But I sent a card."

Sarah opened her mouth and shut it again. She knew something about an attorney's responsibility when there was a trial. You certainly couldn't just tell the judge that you're not going to be there, and you couldn't very well leave your client high and dry. So, there was really nothing she could say to Hannah about her missing her brother's funeral.

She would talk to Ava later on about what would happen if you took off for a funeral when you had a trial, but she knew what Ava was going to say - you have a responsibility to everybody to show up. Still, she noticed the dig that Hannah got in about not understanding anything about work responsibilities. Hannah was poking at her raw spot - that she was a dilettante, a lazy woman of leisure who was a handbag for a rich guy. All of that was accurate, of course, even though Sarah desperately wanted to change that particular narrative.

Sarah decided to turn Hannah's dig back at her. "You had a trial that week, so you couldn't come to your own brother's funeral. So, that tells me you put work above everything else. Yet, you want to raise Julia? What are you going to do, have a nanny raise her?"

Hannah pursed her lips. It was obvious that Sarah managed to poke Hannah's own soft spot. "I'll cut back on my hours," she said. "I'm a partner in my law firm, so I can cut back."

"Oh, okay," Sarah said. "Well, here in California, I'm going to be able to arrange my schedule around Julia. And when I can't watch her, my roommate Quinn can watch her, and when Quinn can't watch her, Mary can. We have a whole village here to raise Julia. What do you have, besides yourself?"

"Really? Are you really going to throw my job in my face?" Hannah rolled her eyes. "Listen, I haven't had the luxury of having a rich guy support me for years. I haven't had the luck of having a very rare penny sent to me and earning me millions of dollars. It's great for you that you have all these wonderful advantages in life, but some of us haven't had those same advantages. Yes, I work for a living. And I'll figure it out. But how dare you throw in my face I work hard for my money?"

Oh, this woman was good. She had the rhetorical gifts of a typical attorney, and, like a typical attorney, she had the singular ability to turn weaknesses into a strength. That's what a good attorney can do – take the weak part of a case, turn it on its head, and make it into a winning argument. It was almost as if this woman knew her major weakness was that she worked a lot, and she came prepared to make her work life her strength in this case. Sarah almost admired Hannah's ability to do this.

Almost.

"I agree," Sarah said. "I've had a lot of advantages in my life. And all of this makes me in a very good position to be raising this child. I do have a flexible job with flexible hours. I'm a partner in a winery, and my sister is my partner. At the moment, my sister Ava is in a position to help me be flexible in the winery business because she doesn't have any responsibilities besides the winery. This means that if Julia has a school function, or she's having boyfriend trouble and needs me, I can be there because I can call on Ava to fill in for me when there's an emergency of some sort. Where will you be if Julia needs you in a pinch?"

Hannah crossed her arms. "I'll have a nanny. Just like your sister had a nanny for her three children when she was working a ton while trying to raise three babies. If you're going to judge me, then maybe you should be looking at your own sister to judge as well."

Sarah knitted her eyebrows. "How do you know so much about my life? And how do you know so much about my sister's life?"

"I'm an attorney. I have an investigator. I make it my job to make sure I know everything about my opponent before I ever set foot into a courtroom. That's what I do. And, at the moment, you're my opponent, so of course I'm going to do opposition research on you. I'm sorry this comes as such a surprise, but it really shouldn't."

Of course. Sarah felt stupid for even asking these questions of Hannah. Apparently, Sarah was an opponent, like she was somebody on the other side of a case. Which she was. She was literally somebody on the other side of the case, and Hannah was going to treat her that way. Sarah knew that when push came to shove, this woman was going to essentially put her on the stand and cross-examine her. Not literally, of course, unless this whole thing ended in a trial and Hannah represented herself.

Sarah nodded her head. It seemed that the two women were playing a game of chess, and Hannah seemed to be perpetually three steps ahead. For every parry, Hannah had a joust. Sarah was up against a master trial attorney, and she was very nervous about that fact.

Sarah stood up again. "Listen, I don't think we're getting anywhere. You've already filed your petition, and now I've accepted service, so I guess it's just a matter of both of us hiring attorneys and going into our respective camps. With the life of a child hanging in the balance."

"That's always how it is in custody cases, isn't it?" Hannah pointedly said. "Two parties go to war, with a child in the middle of all? I don't see how this is any different from any other custody case. Except, of course, the fact that your position is extremely weak. You really don't have any right to custody of Julia. You knew my brother for less than six months, and it's my belief that you and my brother never even consummated your marriage. So your marriage to him really was a sham."

Oh, that one stung. Hannah was right, of course. Sarah never got to know Max enough to actually sleep with him, even though she was married to him. But how did Hannah know this? Surely her crack investigator wasn't going to be able to tell her something like that. And then she realized that Hannah was probably guessing, and psyching her out.

But just because Sarah and Max never slept together

31

didn't mean she didn't love the man. Because she did. She was in love with him. Maybe she didn't know him all that well, but Sarah thought you probably could love somebody you didn't really know. However silly that sounded in her head, she knew it was true. There were definitely feelings she had for Max.

"And now you've crossed the line," Sarah said. "Now, if you'll excuse me, I really need to go. My sister has a very important meeting with the owner of a bakery and catering business who might be able to really give us a real boost with our winery business. And I can't just leave her high and dry. Any more than you could've left your client high and dry when you decided to blow off your own brother's funeral."

Sarah knew she was hitting Hannah below the belt now, but she didn't care. This woman was really working her last nerve. And Hannah was very much putting Sarah off balance, and she didn't like that at all.

Hannah was now standing up. "Okay. I have a flight to catch, anyhow. I'm going back to New York tonight. I have to be back at work tomorrow."

"Wait. You mean to tell me you flew in here just to get me to sign these papers?"

"Correct. I wanted to look you in the eye and tell you that you have no chance. So you might as well give up right now. Yes, I could've taken the easy way out and had a process server give you the papers at some inopportune time for you. But that would not have accomplished what I wanted to accomplish, which was to show you that it's just not any use to even fight this. Julia is going to be in my custody by the end of the year. She will be spending Hanukkah with me in New York City. Mark my words."

Hannah went into the house, apparently to say goodbye to her sister and niece. While she was doing this, Sarah sat on the porch feeling just a little bit punch-drunk. That woman was really a piece of work. She could see why Julia couldn't stand her.

Which was why it was all the harder to know that Hannah was probably right.

Hannah was probably going to get custody of Julia, and there was probably nothing Sarah could do about it. But she was certainly going to try.

She was going to fight like hell. Even if it was for naught, she was going to go to the mattresses.

Julia was just too important.

CHAPTER 5

SARAH

*A*fter Sarah's encounter with the odious Hannah, she knew she had to talk to Mary to get some insight into the woman. She would have to get as much background as possible if she was going to fight this. So, Sarah waited for Hannah to say her rather terse goodbyes to her sister and niece – Hannah was only in the house saying goodbye to Mary and Julia for less than five minutes. Hannah had a flight to catch of course, but that still didn't excuse her dashing away from the place like it had caught fire while she was in the living room.

As soon as Hannah left, Sarah went into Mary's house. Mary and Julia were sitting in the living room. Mary was comforting Julia, as Julia's head was on Mary's shoulder. The girl was still sobbing, and there were boxes of Kleenex all over the coffee table.

Mary motioned to Sarah to sit down next to them on the couch. "Tell me how it went," she said to Sarah.

"Horrible. That woman is a real piece of work. At the same time, she's strangely persuasive. As she should be, because she's a trial attorney. The woman knows how to go for the jugular, that's for sure."

Mary nodded her head. "That's putting it mildly. And her ability to go for the jugular won't make her a good parent or guardian. I tried to tell her this before she came here to do this. I told her not to bother."

Sarah raised her eyebrows. "So you knew this was brewing."

"Yes. I did," Mary said. "And I should have warned you. But I didn't think she was serious. That's how naïve I am. I had no idea she would actually go through with this. Because after all, she doesn't know Julia at all. She's barely seen her. And let's just say that she vehemently disapproved of the fact that Julia was-"

Mary shook her head. "Julia, why don't you to see what Emerson's doing? See if you can maybe go over there. I'll call Quinn and see if she can't pick you up and take you over to her house."

Julia nodded. "I get it. You guys want to talk without me being around. I think it's a good idea. I'll give Emerson a call."

Julia went into the other room and called Emerson. That she came back out five minutes later. "Quinn's going to come get me in 10 minutes. She's working from home today."

That was the good thing about Quinn's interior decorating business. There were many days when she was working from home, because she had a thriving e-design business in addition to doing the on-site work. Quinn could work with people around the world with the e-design part of her business. How she worked her e-design part of her business was that the client would send her pictures and measurements of their homes, and Quinn would send them design concepts and a personalized shopping list. Quinn typically did her e-design business two days a week, and her on-site business, which was much more lucrative, three or four days a week. This allowed her to be flexible with the care of the girls.

Mary just took a deep breath and waited for Quinn to show up to take Julia away. Sarah and Mary both knew that Julia needed Emerson. Emerson could relate so much to Julia. They both were essentially orphaned, and they both ended up living with a woman they barely knew. In Emerson's case, she was living with her actual birth mother, because Quinn had given up Emerson initially for adoption. When Emerson's adoptive parents both died, she ended up with Quinn, her birth mother. As for Julia, this was the situation she was in – living with Sarah, her stepmother, but it wasn't so bad because Emerson was her best friend, and she lived under the same roof as Emerson, and her aunt was just down the street in Malibu.

Quinn showed up about 10 minutes later. She came into the house, and Sarah briefly told her what was going on. Sarah didn't tell her too much, just that Julia's aunt was fighting for custody. Quinn's eyes got wide and she put her hand to her heart. "Oh my heck, I can't believe that. This can't be happening, can it?"

"I wish it weren't," Sarah said. "But it is."

Julia was motioning to Quinn that she wanted to leave. "I'll call you later about this," Quinn said. "I really hope this doesn't happen."

"You and me both," Sarah said.

Quinn and Julia left, and then Sarah and Mary picked up the conversation where they dropped it. "You were saying something about Hannah," Sarah said. "Something about her vehemently opposing something regarding Julia."

Mary took a deep breath. "Yes. And I almost said it in front of Julia. Sometimes my big mouth gets me in trouble.

But what I was going to say was that Hannah vehemently opposed to Julia even being born. She said it was unnatural. She said it was against God's will or something of the sort. But Max's wife Elaine wanted it. She wanted desperately to have a child when she was alive. And then when she got cancer, she told my brother Max that it was important to her to have a legacy."

"And what did Max think about it at first?" Sarah asked.

"At first, he didn't want to do it," Mary said. "But then he told me that he wanted something from Elaine, who he loved so desperately. He wanted her to live on through a child. So that was why he decided to go ahead and have a surrogate give birth to Julia."

"So Hannah was against it?"

"Yes," Mary said. "She was. Hannah was always much more religious than either me or Max. Especially me. I've never been religious at all, to tell you the truth. Max, of course, was religious. But he was more a follower of Reform Judaism. He was much more into bringing his religion into today's society. Hannah is much more into Orthodox Judaism."

Sarah nodded. She was aware of the different sects of Judaism. Reform Judaism was considered progressive, and the adherents of that sect of Judaism were more focused on the ethical aspects of the religion and the changing nature of society and how the changing society fit with the religion. Orthodox Judaism was much like Evangelical Christianity, in that it regarded the Torah as the revealed word of God, therefore the Torah was to be taken literally and not strayed from.

"I see. So, I assume that if Julia goes to live with Hannah, she will be forced into observing Orthodox Judaism," Sarah said. "It would be like taking somebody who's a member of a progressive Episcopalian church and forcing them to go to an Evangelical church."

Mary shook her head sorrowfully. "Yes. That's true. That's a very good analogy. Because Hannah isn't somebody who allows free thinking under her roof. She thinks every-body must bend to her will and think like her. If you don't bend to her will and think like her, you're clearly wrong, and she'll force you to think like her. I'm not just talking about religion, either. I'm talking about every aspect of her life."

Sarah really started to fear for Julia as she talked to Mary. Julia was very fragile, especially at that moment when she just lost her father. She was a sensitive girl, and, unlike Emerson, Julia was somebody who wouldn't make waves. Which meant that if she lived with a controlling person, she could never find the person she really was. She could be molded into a girl she never thought she would be and never wanted to be. That was a scary thought for Sarah, because Sarah had been in that kind of situation herself with the controlling Nolan.

"So, for instance?" Sarah asked.

"For instance, Hannah would probably insist that Julia follow her into the field of law," Mary said. "She would prob-ably never give Julia the chance to find her own path. Julia loves to write poetry, and Hannah has told me to my face that I should discourage her from writing poetry, because it's a waste of time. To Hannah, hobbies in general are a waste of time. I don't even need to tell you how much she disapproves of my lifestyle. I'm working as an artist, and in Hannah's world, artists have no place. She doesn't appreciate beauty or art or music or any of that. She only appreciates the almighty dollar and her very intolerant views about who's productive and good and who isn't."

Mary went over to the window and looked out of it. "She's really throwing it in my face that I don't have the

38

means to take care of Julia myself. I think that's why she's doing this, you know. She wants me to know that my life-style of living off my art, which isn't much of a living at all because I'm not exactly successful in selling my paintings, is unacceptable. I could be much more successful in selling my art if I were more of a business person, which I'm not. I'm not good at all with marketing and networking and every-thing you need to do to become successful in my field. And she wants to punish me for choosing this life. That's why she wants to take Julia away from me and from you. She wants me to somehow conform to what she wants me to be."

"I don't understand?" Sarah said.

Mary turned from the window. "She flat-out told me that if I gave up working as an artist that she would drop the custody issue. She wants me to go back to what I was doing before, which was working as a corporate lawyer. She told me that if I went back to that field, she would allow Julia to live with me."

Sarah scrunched her eyebrows. "You were a corporate lawyer?"

"Yes, I was," Mary said. "For only five years, though. I haven't been a lawyer for over 30 years. When I met my husband Isaac, I gave it up. He inspired me to give up law. He knew I wasn't happy being a lawyer, and that I had the soul of an artist, and that was that. I became a professional artist and I never looked back."

Wow, Sarah thought. She looked at the woman in front of her, with the pink streaks running through her gray hair, and she really couldn't place her in any kind of a law office. "I'm sorry, I'm having a hard time picturing you in a courtroom."

Mary laughed ruefully. "Well, I never actually got into a courtroom, so maybe that's why you could never imagine me trying a case. I did the grunt work for the law firm, and I wasn't very good, so I never rose above the grunt work. I was always doing research for the partners. Sometimes I would write a brief. I did discovery requests and document review and reviewed discovery responses from opposing counsel. It was boring, soul-crushing work."

"You sound like my sister Ava," Sarah said with a laugh. "She was in that same boat, although she was pretty high-up with her law firm even if she never did make partner."

Mary smiled. "The entire time I was working for that firm, and I mean the entire time, I was dreaming of doing something else. In my heart I was always an artist, but I never believed I could be successful. My Isaac, he showed me that I really needed to live my truth, because if I didn't, I would become a bitter woman who was never able to break out into the life I wanted. He was an artist, too. He was never successful, either. Thank God he inherited this house. Otherwise I don't know how we would've lived once the savings ran out. I did managed to save quite a bit from my corporate law job, but that only went so far. So we lived hand to mouth, but we were so happy. We were living out our dreams of being professional artists, and nothing could replace that."

"And Hannah wants you to go back to law, even though you weren't happy doing that?"

"Yes," Mary said. "Hannah has been pestering me ever since I left my corporate law job to go back. I can't tell you how many Thanksgiving dinners she's ruined because she would spend the entire meal time attacking me for my choice of leaving law to become an artist. And she has never been able to let that go. So, now, she has her chance to force me into the life she wants for me. She's trying to use Julia as a bargaining chip, and that's all Julia is to her. Julia is a means to an end, and that end is me going back into corporate law."

"Wow. What did she think about Max becoming a farmer?"

Mary laughed. "She didn't approve, of course. She really

couldn't understand why Max would leave a high-powered political consulting job to live on a farm."

"But he inherited that farm from your father, right?"

Mary laughed again. "No, no. He just told everybody that the farm had been in his family for generations, because it sounded much more romantic somehow. You know, he comes from a long line of farmers, he told everybody. People prefer to deal with somebody who's a legacy farmer, which was what he told everybody he was. But, no, our father did not leave him that farm."

"What did your father do?"

"He drove a truck locally," Mary said. "Our mother was a nursery school teacher. My mother was insanely happy doing what she was doing, even if the pay was bubkus. Our father was happy doing what he was doing, too, even though he didn't make a lot of money, either. They both were doing what they wanted to do, and money was always tight growing up."

"And how did Hannah react to growing up middle-class?"

"Working class, really," Mary said. "And Hannah was always disgusted with our parents. Always. She always demanded things my parents couldn't afford to give her, like new cars and European vacations and things like that. Obviously, she never got those things from our parents, and she always howled about how unfair they were being. We lived in New York City, anyhow, right in Manhattan, so nobody we knew had a car and it was always pointless to have one in the city. So, our parents didn't buy her a car when she turned 16, and she didn't speak to either of them for the better part of a year because of it."

"What do you mean, she didn't speak to them? She lived under the same roof, didn't she?" Sarah asked.

"Yes, which is what made it all so crazy. She literally didn't speak a word to them for almost a year. They'd ask her questions and she would act like she was mute or something. She wrote her responses on a sheet of paper or asked me to give the message to our parents."

"Didn't she understand your parents couldn't afford to buy her a car or that a car was impractical?" Sarah asked.

"Yes, of course she understood this," Mary said. "But she couldn't stand the unfairness of it all. She just thought that all 16-year-olds were entitled to a brand new car and extended European vacations. She never lived in the real world. She hated our parents just because they couldn't provide for her the way she wanted them to."

"That was the reason why she became a high-powered lawyer," Sarah said.

Mary nodded. "That was the reason why she became a high-powered lawyer," she confirmed. "She's one of the top five attorneys in the city, you know. Makes over $1 million a year. Has a gorgeous apartment on the Upper West side, facing the park. And she throws all that in my face, too. And, believe me, she hates that I have this beautiful home in Malibu. I didn't earn this home, she's always telling me. How dare I have a home worth $2 million when I was such a loser in my career?"

"So, if Julia goes to live with her..."

Mary grimaced. "Yes. Julia is going to be raised with Hannah's values, Hannah's rigidity, Hannah's controlling nature. Julia will have no choice but to become a mini version of Hannah. If she doesn't, Hannah will make her life a living hell. So, in a matter of years, my niece will be somebody I don't know. She's not going to be the sweet, poetic, sensitive, intelligent and artistic soul she is. She's going to become mean, controlling, and materialistic like my sister."

Mary started to cry. Sarah went over to her and put her arms around her.

"Won't the judge see all this?" Sarah asked. "Take this all

into account? Surely the judge will understand that it's in Julia's best interest to stay with people who are going to nurture her basic nature and not try to change her into somebody she's not."

"I would hope so, but who knows what a judge will do?" Mary said ruefully. "Unfortunately, Hannah has the upper hand from the get-go, because she's family and you're not." She started to pace around the room. "God, I wish I had the money to raise her properly. If I did, I'd put this entire thing to rest and take Julia under my own roof to raise. But Hannah would still fight me for custody, because like I said, she told me that she would only give up her petition for custody if I did what she said and went back into corporate law."

" Your parents, were they very religious?" Sarah asked. "I'm just curious."

"Yes, they were," Mary said. "They were conservative Jews, but not Orthodox. They followed all the rabbinical laws. We kept kosher at our home, very solemnly observed the sabbath, observed all the holidays and went through all the rituals. Hannah decided on her own to become Orthodox, which is her choice, of course. But she really thought my brother was a heathen for being a member of such a progressive temple and when I told her I abandoned religion entirely, she almost decided never to speak to me again."

Sarah nodded. "Damn. I wish there was some way you could go ahead and take Julia. But I know you can't afford it."

"I know," Mary said. "Ever since Hannah called me to tell me she was going to do this, I've been thinking the same thing. Don't get me wrong, I'm happy doing what I'm doing. I love my work. I look forward to every single day, because I know every day I'm going to create something new with my hands and my brain and my canvas. And I so want Julia to have that same opportunity to self-actualize. I want her to explore what she wants to do in life and go for it, whatever it is. She's an amazing song-writer and loves to bake. She could pursue either of those fields, or maybe something different. Activism or something. Whatever she wants out of life, she can go for it. That's what I want for her. And that's exactly what Hannah won't give her."

It was Sarah's turn to stand up and start pacing around the room. "What judge is going to prefer a rando like me over a close blood relation like Hannah when it comes to custody? The only thing I can possibly count on is the judge will look at the best interest of Julia and see she's obviously better off with me. But I just don't trust the legal system."

Sarah was unable to trust the legal system ever since she was in the system herself. When she was facing a drug charge, when she took the rap for her former friend Lauren's drugs, and she had to plead guilty because if she didn't she probably would've been found guilty at trial, she lost faith in the legal system. She came to see the legal system as being oppressive and not being interested at all in facts. She was jaded when it came to the law. So she was really cynical when she thought about the possibility that she would prevail in a custody battle with Hannah. She knew in her heart that she wouldn't.

She felt tears coming to her own eyes now. Julia in this case was nothing but a pawn. She was a tool for Hannah to try to force her sister into a life she didn't want. And she didn't want to take Julia because she loved her and wanted what was best for her. No. She wanted Julia because she wanted somebody whose life she could ruin. She could apparently never bend her parents to her will, and she couldn't bend her siblings to her will, either. So she was going to take an impressionable young girl who just lost her father, a young girl who wasn't strong-willed, and mold her into her own mini-me.

It was disgusting, using a child like that. Hannah apparently didn't care that she was going to ruin Julia's life. The only thing she cared about was control and power.

And the sad thing was, she would probably win in court.

Sarah saw no way around it.

CHAPTER 6

QUINN

*W*hen Quinn got Julia from Mary's home, Julia immediately went to the beach, because that's where Emerson was, as Emerson was surfing on that day. Emerson was part of a group led by older surfing instructors, so Quinn wasn't worried about the two girls hanging out on the beach by themselves.

Quinn was very worried about Julia. Mainly, she was worried that Julia would end up moving to New York City to live with her Aunt Hannah. She was starting to become very fond of the young girl, but that wasn't the reason why she was worried. She was worried because Julia was a very grounding influence on her own daughter Emerson.

Emerson was a handful for a variety of reasons. One of the main reasons why she was so difficult to manage was because she was so darned intelligent. That, combined with the fact that she was extremely high strung, made for a headstrong, stubborn, energetic young lady who chafed against any rules or structures. Emerson calmed down a bit when she was working for Ava's bed-and-breakfast, entertaining the patrons with her exquisite violin playing. That gave her an outlet for her creativity and her passions, and she really seemed to enjoy it. And, for once, Emerson seemed to be a little bit tamed.

Just a little. What *really* tamed her was her friendship with Julia. While Emerson was certainly a young girl who knew her own mind who was not going to march to the beat of anybody's drummer, Julia, with her calm demeanor and love of faith, intrigued Emerson and seemed to calm Emerson down quite a bit. Emerson, like Quinn's friends Ava and Sarah, was becoming interested in Judaism. But her interest in the religion was only superficial. She wasn't interested in learning Hebrew or having a Bat Mitzvah, even though Julia just had hers the previous month.

What Emerson was actually interested in was the Jewish emphasis on social justice and good works. Julia was very focused on that aspect of her religion. Emerson had always been into causes. Whether it was environmental, political, feminist, or LGBTQ rights, Emerson was always there, writing letters to newspapers, keeping up a blog, calling her state senators and representatives, and speaking to her students in the school.

Emerson had also recently announced to Quinn that she'd become a vegan. Not that that was a surprise to Quinn. The only surprise was that Emerson wasn't a vegan before this. After all, Emerson was very into climate change and environmental causes. She'd been pestering Quinn to get solar panels for their new Venice Beach house, and Quinn agreed. And then she started to pester Quinn about buying an electric car.

" But don't buy a Tesla," she said to Quinn. "That Elon Musk dude's rank. He's all up the authoritarians' asses, he won't pay his fair share of taxes, and he's just weird."

Quinn actually agreed with Emerson's characterization of Elon Musk. The dude *was* weird, with his 80 gajillion children and multiple baby mamas, his constant bellyaching about having to pay taxes even though he's worth over $300 billion, and his kissing the asses of Vladimir Putin and Xi Jinping, the leader of China. Quinn also didn't agree with Elon Musk when it came to the issue of Twitter. Quinn was monitoring her daughter's Twitter feed, and she couldn't believe some of the foul and vile things she saw on that site. The place was a cesspool of misinformation and disinformation, and that was with a little bit of content moderation. Musk has declared that he wanted ideas to flow freely, no matter how based on lies these ideas were, so he wanted less content moderation. Quinn saw that idea as ridiculous - the guy wanted even more sewage and lies to flow through that site?

So, it didn't take much convincing from Emerson that Quinn should not give Elon Musk a dime. She also agreed with Emerson that it was time to buy an electric car. Not just because of the environmental concerns, although she was concerned about climate change and the environment. She always had been concerned about these things, and now, having a young daughter who would have to live with the environment Quinn's generation was leaving, she was more concerned than ever. But she was also looking forward to not having to pay over six dollars a gallon for gas.

"Yeah, mom, we need to get off fossil fuels," Emerson said to Quinn. "We got too many dictators around the world holding this nation by the nut sack just because we need their dirty oil. We got dirty people doing dirty deeds because we need their dirty fuel." And then Emerson proceeded to tell Quinn all about how Saudi Arabia, in league with Russia, used the price of oil to weaken this country to return the people they want back to power.

So, Quinn ended up buying a Cadillac Lyriq SUV, a sleek, stylish car that got over 300 miles per charge. It was a beautiful car in a candy apple red with leather seats, satellite radio, the works. It cost a lot of money to buy that car, but Quinn felt she worked so hard that she deserved to splurge once in a great while.

Quinn was really starting to see Julia's influence rub off on Emerson. Emerson was so less wild than she used to be, so much more focused on positive things. Emerson no longer wanted to do things like sneak out of the house to join groups of kids who were much older than herself on the beach. She and Julia were like two peas in a pod, surfing together on the weekends, volunteering together at a local animal shelter, and hanging out in their shared room, just being teenagers.

They were even starting to embark on another project, which was songwriting. Emerson was a wonderful violinist, and she'd been interested in composing music since she was a young girl of only five years old. She was ready to start composing pop music, but she didn't have the knack for lyrics. Turned out Julia did have the knack for lyrics, as she was a poet in her spare time. So, the two girls spent hours in their room, writing songs together. They performed these songs for Quinn and her friends, and they all thought that they were quite good.

No doubt about it, the two girls were as tight as can be. So Quinn knew that if Julia had to move away to New York City, Emerson would be absolutely devastated. Quinn worried about what Emerson would do if she lost her other half.

Before she and Julia became best friends, Emerson was a much different child. She was unfocused, to say the least. Because of Emerson's penchant for sneaking out of the house to hang out with older kids, Quinn worried that Emerson would go down a bad path with bad people.

Meeting Julia at the middle school on Nantucket changed

all that. Julia was the one who focused Emerson's energies on causes. And causes was the one thing that focused Emerson on positive aspects of life. She was no longer channeling her energies towards running wild, but towards agitating for a better world.

So Quinn knew she would have to do everything in her power to make sure that Julia stayed right there in Malibu.

In the meantime, Quinn decided it would be helpful for Emerson and Julia if they could have the help of a professional songwriter. After listening to the girls' lyrics and music, Quinn knew that the girls were going for a bit of a Tori Amos vibe. Like Tori Amos, the girls were composing piano-backed songs based upon somewhat obscure and metaphorical lyrics focused on feminist, societal and relationship issues. Many of the lyrics focused on grief, as well, as Julia was still struggling to come to terms with the recent death of her father and the fact that she literally never knew her birth mother. Julia was born to a surrogate after her birth mother died of cancer. Before Julia's birth mother died of cancer, she and Max, Julia's father, froze some fertilized embryos that were then implanted in a surrogate and that was how Julia was born.

Quinn was also surprised that Emerson was able to play the piano. She found this out when Emerson asked Quinn to buy a baby grand piano, and Ava agreed to this request. Ava's sunroom was not yet furnished, so that would be a perfect place to put a baby grand piano.

Emerson sat down to the piano, and she immediately was able to play. "Don't look so surprised," Emerson said when Quinn watched her daughter playing the piano with an astonished look on her face. "You know I'm able to play music by ear. And I learned about playing the piano from watching Deacon all those Saturday nights. And, dude, if Julia and me are going to set the world on fire with our songwriting, I have to get good on the piano. Whoever heard of a singer-songwriter whose main instrument is the violin?"

Deacon was the man who played the piano at Ava's bed and breakfast on Saturday nights. He also became Ava's main squeeze for a while, before he went back to Australia to attend to his sick sister who was stricken with cancer for the second time. Every Saturday night, Deacon played the piano for Ava's customers while Emerson played the violin.

So, Quinn decided to hire a professional songwriter who could guide the girls. She wasn't quite sure exactly where to begin with her search for the perfect songwriting mentor, but she knew a good place to start would be Morgan, who was Hallie's daughter. Morgan owned an art gallery cooperative in Venice Beach. Since she was a part of the artistic community, Quinn thought there would be a chance that Morgan might know somebody who would fit the bill.

So she headed over to Morgan's art gallery to talk to the young artist.

In the back of Quinn's mind, she thought that the whole prospect of Julia becoming a songwriter in Los Angeles would be enough to keep her in town. Surely Julia's Aunt Hannah wouldn't be so selfish as to take her niece away from a promising hobby and maybe future career, not to mention taking her away from her best friend and her village of adults who were willing and able to take care of the young girl.

Would she?

CHAPTER 7

QUINN

Quinn got to Morgan's art gallery and walked in. She'd never been in this gallery yet, but she was very impressed by it. She walked around and admired all the paintings on the wall, looking for Morgan.

Morgan finally appeared about half an hour after Quinn got to the gallery. She apparently had been on a Starbucks run, as she had several coffees and pastries in her hands for everybody. "Hey, Quinn," she said in a friendly manner. She kissed Quinn on the cheek. "What's going on?"

"I was wondering if you knew anybody who's a singer-songwriter who might be able to mentor a couple of very young girls," Quinn said. "My daughter and her best friend who lives with us have been messing around, getting some songs together. I think they have a lot of potential. So I wanted to find somebody who's a professional and kinda knows the ropes who might be able to take them under her wing, for a fee, of course."

Morgan smiled. "What kind of music are they composing?" She asked.

"Kinda an alternative vibe," Quinn said. "Think Tori

Amos, Kate Bush, Sarah McLachlan, Florence + the Machine, that sort of genre."

"Oh, kind of the artsy fartsy deep poetic kind of music? If that's the case, I have the perfect person for you. Her name is Mia Artemis. She's not a singer, but she's a very good song- writer. She's sold a lot of her songs, and her lyrics are the bomb."

Quinn blinked. "Oh my God. Did she live in New York in the late '80s?" Even as Quinn asked that, she knew the answer. Of course Mia had lived in New York in the late '80s. Quinn actually knew the woman when she first moved to New York. She was living in a hovel in Bensonhurst, and Mia lived down the hall. Benjamin, her husband, was always gone, because he was working a lot at a restaurant, and Quinn was left home alone almost every night.

She had not yet found her footing at that time. She didn't really know what to do with her life. She only knew herself as being Benjamin's wife, and Benjamin was never around for her. So she and Mia hung out quite a few nights, just drinking beer out of a bottle and hanging out on Quinn's fire escape, listening to the constant sounds of sirens and talking about life until dawn.

Then about a year after Quinn had moved into the apart- ment and had gotten to know Mia, Mia had announced that she was moving to Los Angeles to pursue a songwriting career. Quinn was really sorry to see her go, because she was lonely without Benjamin being around. And she really enjoyed the conversations she and Mia had all the time.

Mia was always playing her guitar and singing. Some- times she was a street performer, with an open guitar case where people could throw dollar bills. Other times, she actu- ally managed to get real gigs at local coffee shops. Quinn saw her a time or two at various venues, and she thought she really had a knack for writing songs. Her performances were always very popular with the coffeehouse set and she even managed to get quite a few people throwing money into her guitar case when she was singing on the street. Quinn was very impressed by that, because she always believed that people rarely donated to street performers, yet Mia usually came home with $100 or more after a good night on the street.

Mia was really her first close girlfriend, the kind of person that one knows in their early 20s when life was so full of possibility and you didn't really have a chance to become jaded yet. It was a time of her life when she was looking for a chosen family, having moved away from her own flesh and blood family. And, considering this was not quite the era of texting and emails, it was very easy to lose touch with people when they move across the country.

So, even though the two women had promised one another they wouldn't lose touch, that's exactly what happened. Mia became really engrossed in the Los Angeles life, and Quinn was still stuck in the depressing Bensonhurst apartment, perpetually waiting for Benjamin to come home from his restaurant job, and they just didn't talk to each other anymore.

And now, she was going to reconnect with Mia. How strange life was sometimes. How small the world was. She felt a little excited about seeing her old friend. She always wondered what happened to Mia along the line. She hated that the two of them had completely lost touch, but she just thought it was one of those things – people leave an imprint on your heart, and then they are gone, but you are forever changed. And that's how she felt about Mia.

Mia had filled a void in her life when she desperately needed somebody, anybody, to take an interest in her. She really thought she made a mistake moving to New York, because she didn't want to. She only moved to New York because Benjamin wanted to, without regard for her feelings or for what she might do in that city. He just didn't care, because he had his career and he was selfish. He was so busy trying to get ahead that he didn't even think about his wife at home who was bored and depressed, even more depressed after Mia had left.

"Yeah, I think she lived in New York City in the late 80s," Morgan said. "She said she was a native New Yorker. At any rate, I think she'd be perfect for what you're wanting to do. I know she makes a good living as a songwriter."

"That would be great. Tell you what, why don't you give me her phone number, and I'll give her a call."

"I can do one better. We're having another one of our wine and cheese parties tomorrow night. Mia is going to be here. If you're free, maybe you can stop by."

Quinn took a deep breath. Man, all of a sudden, she was so excited to see her old friend. She wondered what she looked like. It'd been over 30 years since the two women had laid eyes on one another. She was really anxious to find out how the past 30 years had treated her old friend. She wondered if she was happy in a relationship, and if she was doing very well with her career. She seemed to remember that Mia swung both ways back in the day, for she dated both men and women openly. She wondered if Mia had settled on a lane, or if she was still straddling both lines.

That was another thing Quinn was thinking about. Mia was always very attractive to her. She was so different from anybody she'd ever known in her small town in Georgia. Mia, with her tattoo sleeve, her ripped jeans, leather jacket, Doc Martens and Mohawk dyed bright pink, was at once free-spirited and androgynous. If ever there was a hall pass for Quinn back in the day, it would've been Mia.

She never would've cheated on Benjamin, even with a woman, but, during their long talks on the fire escape, Quinn

55

was sorely tempted to. Mia was very beautiful, with crystalline blue eyes, high cheekbones, and a beautiful Roman nose. Her face was so delicate, which completely contrasted with the rest of her bad ass get up. It was almost funny.

"Oh, I'll be here," Quinn said. "Don't worry about that."

As she drove away from the art gallery, Quinn felt an excitement she hadn't felt in awhile. She was going to see Mia Artemis again, at long last.

At the same time, she felt a sense of confusion. Back then, she didn't really know who she was or what she was going to be. She was married to a man who was never home, living in a slum in Bensonhurst, which, at that time, was an enclave filled with gang violence and racial tension. She desperately needed a lifeline, and that's what Mia was, but there was also an undercurrent of sexual tension between the two of them.

At that time, Quinn was not yet the confident woman she was. She was more of a confused girl from a small town in Georgia, and she was definitely like Alice in Wonderland, coming into a scary landscape that she didn't quite know how to navigate. Her feelings for Mia at the time were not quite formed and were scary for her. They were scary for her because she was married to Benjamin, even if Benjamin wasn't ever around and really wasn't a husband to her. They were also scary for her because she didn't think she could be with a woman.

So, while the prospect of seeing Mia again filled her with joy, there was also an apprehension. Would she have the same feelings for Mia that she did back then? She didn't really know.

But she was about to find out.

CHAPTER 8

QUINN

*A*fter Quinn had visited Morgan and got information about her old friend Mia Artemis, she went home and found that the girls were in the house, baking sugar-free cookies.

Julia was like Quinn in that she was very health-conscious, and she didn't like to eat a lot of sugar. She apparently had seen a documentary about the issue of sugar and what it does to your body on Netflix, and, after seeing that, she decided to give it up.

The documentary she watched was called *That Sugar Film,* and it followed one man who, before the documentary was shot, didn't eat sugar at all, but for the purposes of the documentary, he ate a lot of sugar every day for 60 days. Actually, the amount of sugar he ate every day for the 60 days was equivalent to what the average person in a developed country would eat. The result was that he gained a lot of weight, got a fatty liver and lost a lot of his energy. In only 60 days!

Julia told Quinn that after she saw that film she decided to give up sugar. And, she was very careful to make sure that she didn't eat a lot of things that had hidden sugar, such as ketchup and barbecue sauce and things like that.

Julia was apparently rubbing off on Emerson, as Emerson, like Julia, decided to cut sugar out of her diet as well, even sugar that came from fruit. Which complicated matters for Quinn a little, because Emerson was also a vegan, so it was difficult to understand exactly what Emerson could eat. But, Quinn being Quinn, she was able to figure out what she could feed her daughter. Basically, Emerson was eating a vegan keto diet, which seemed like a contradiction in terms to Quinn at first. Quinn knew quite a bit about the keto diet, and knew it was a high-fat low-carb moderate protein diet. And most people on this diet ate a lot of animal protein.

Quinn found several vegan keto diet cookbooks, and Emerson and Julia really were excited about these cookbooks, especially Julia, who was really a natural cook. She told Quinn that she'd been cooking since she was five years old. At that time, she was only making things like scrambled eggs and pancakes, but she learned much more along the way, and, because there wasn't a mother in the house and her father disliked cooking, Julia eventually became the main cook in their house. She was still very interested in cooking and had even taken a cooking class. She enjoyed watching cooking shows and reading recipe books and she loved to try out different recipes that she would see on the cooking shows and read in the recipe books.

One of the things that Emerson and Julia really loved to make were sugar-free vegan chocolate chip cookies. They were made with cashew butter, sweetener, egg substitute, and keto chocolate chips. And that's what Julia and Emerson were making when Quinn came in the door after talking to Morgan. Quinn really loved the smell of baking cookies, and she really was happy that Emerson was finally eating healthy things she made for herself.

Emerson really had come a long way from the days when she came to Quinn's house, wanting only to eat junk food. She apparently had grown up on frozen waffles and Doritos, or at least that was the way she described her diet before coming to live with Quinn. Quinn had to trick her into eating healthy by sneaking in vegetables and fruits into junk food – such as making pudding made of avocado, or macaroni and cheese made with butternut squash in the mix.

Now, here Emerson was, seeking out healthy sugar-free recipes, and Quinn couldn't be prouder.

Quinn smelled the delicious cookies, and she knew they were delicious because Emerson and Julia had made them before, and she immediately went to the refrigerator and got out some almond milk so she could have milk and cookies.

The first batch came out and cooled on the cookie rack that was placed on the island in the large kitchen. Emerson offered Quinn a hot cookie, and Quinn eagerly nodded her head and got out a plate. Emerson put several cookies on that plate.

As Quinn bit into the delicious cookie that tasted so nutty and buttery and sweet that you could never tell it was healthy, Quinn was taken back to her childhood. Her mother would bake her chocolate chip cookies that were amazing right out of the oven with a glass of regular milk. Now, the cookies were flour free and sugar free, and the milk was made out of almonds, as Quinn was unable to process regular milk anymore, but the cookies and the milk were just as good as Quinn remembered from her childhood.

" You girls should start your own cooking show," Quinn said as she ate the cookies and milk. "Or open up your own Keto vegan bakery."

Emerson just rolled her eyes. "Dude, that's not happening. But I admit, I do love to make these things." And then she looked over at Julia, who was busy getting out some more ingredients from the fridge. Emerson put her head down and said in a very low voice "Julia likes to do a lot of baking when she's pissed. So you're going to be eating keto vegan brownies, cakes, and pies for a while."

Julia came back over to Quinn and Emerson. "Emerson, I heard every word you said. And, you're right. I'm going to become a baking fiend from here on out. Too bad we're not in school because I could supply baking fund drives from here on out."

"Well, I'm sure that Sarah and Ava could use these beauties at their new winery," Quinn said. "Baked goods go really well with wine."

"Good," Julia said. "That means I don't have the throw most of my baked goods in the trash."

Quinn leaned forward. She was a bit concerned that Sarah was not back yet from Mary's house. She knew that wasn't necessarily a good sign, because Sarah was obviously still talking to Mary. And if she'd been talking to her for this long, and it had been hours, the entire situation with Julia's custody was probably complicated, to say the least. She was very anxious to talk to Sarah to find out exactly what was going on. She was on pins and needles about it.

"Julia," Quinn said. "Do you know what's going on?"

Julia had another tray of cookies coming out of the oven. She grabbed the tray of cookies and slammed them down on the counter. "No. But I know that if I have to go to live with that woman, I'm going to lose my mind." She shook her head. "And I know she's up to no good. She doesn't love me. She hardly even knows me. Sarah doesn't know me either, but Sarah cares to get to know me. Not my Aunt Hannah. I've lived my whole life knowing that woman, and she has never once asked me one question about my life. She's just horrible."

Emerson gave Quinn a look that told Quinn that she was

to step lightly around Julia right now. Quinn was amused that Emerson, of all people, was apparently cowed by Julia's mood. Quinn never knew Emerson to get cowed by anything or anybody. Yet, apparently Emerson at that moment was trying to walk on eggshells around her best friend. That told Quinn everything she needed to know. Well, that and the fact that the kitchen was filled with the smell of cookies and brownies.

Julia took a baking dish full of brownies out of the oven and put them in front of Quinn, who took one of the brownies, and bit into it. It was chewy and sweet and the melty and delectable. She was amazed that this brownie, like the chocolate chip cookies, was made without sugar or flour.

She was thinking that the girls had a bright future with the songwriting, but if that didn't pan out, they could have a future baking healthy treats. Julia really was an amazing baker, and Emerson wasn't bad herself.

"Julia, don't even worry about it until we know what's going on," Quinn said to Julia as she took another bite out of her brownie.

Emerson rolled her eyes. "Not helping, mom. If Julia is going to stress out about this, she's going to stress out about it. There's nothing you can say to get her to not stress out about it, so don't even try. And please don't give her some kind of rank speech about how she can adjust if she goes to New York City, because she's not gonna adjust. So don't even think about it. Just let her do her baking and she's probably going to write a poem or two or maybe some song lyrics, and that's how she's gonna deal with it. Telling her not to worry about it is not helping."

Quinn knew the truth of Emerson's words. When somebody was stressed out about something as major as what Julia might have to face - moving across the country to live with an aunt who couldn't care less about her – there really was no use in telling a person "just don't worry about it." Obviously, she was going to worry about it, and Quinn telling her not to worry about it was just dismissive and wrong. Quinn felt chastened and embarrassed that she said those words to Julia about Julia not worrying until she knew more.

"You're right, Emerson, as usual." Then she looked at Julia. "What are your feelings about this?"

"I'm angry, scared, and feel so helpless," Julia said as she arranged more sugar-free chocolate chips, almond flour, almond milk and baking soda on the counter. "I've lost everything. I have no more family left, except for my Aunt Mary. No blood family, although I know that Sarah will try her best to become my mom. I'm really happy being here in California, close to my aunt and my best friend. And Hannah wants to take that away because she's just that selfish."

"Sugar, I wish I had words for you," Quinn said. "But I don't. And I won't. I'm not going to lie to you and tell you there's no way your aunt can get custody of you, because I know that's not true. She's your aunt, your blood relation. And a judge is going to take that into consideration. I'm assuming that Sara will be at a disadvantage because she's not a blood relation."

There. Quinn told Julia the awful truth, which was that Julia had a good chance of going with her aunt. She hated telling Julia the truth, but she also knew young girl already knew that truth.

Julia didn't react to Quinn speaking so bluntly, except to go over to the stove and melt some baking chocolate in a double boiler. "I'm going to make lava cake," she announced. "With espresso. I'm making this because I really love it, and I know that if I go to live with Hannah, I'm not going to be able to bake anything. So, I might as well get all the baking in that I can."

Quinn looked at Emerson, who shrugged her shoulders. "Why will Hannah not allow you to bake?"

"Because it's a waste of time," Julia said in a high-pitched exaggerated voice that told Quinn that Julia was mocking Hannah. " My whole life is going to be spent reading legal briefs and law books when I'm not forced to do a million hours of homework every night for classes that I don't care about. Doing things like baking and writing poems are a waste of time to Hannah. She's going to force me to become a lawyer, I just know it."

Quinn wanted to tell her she was being a dramatic teenager who was looking at the worst-case scenario as if that was sure to happen, but she kept her mouth shut. She hadn't yet talked to Sarah, so she had no idea if Julia was right about her Aunt Hannah. It was entirely possible that Julia wasn't exaggerating and that Hannah really was that controlling. Quinn couldn't discount that possibility, so she didn't say a word.

"Julia, I really wish I had something to say to you, sugar," Quinn said gently. "But I can tell you that I have some good news for you. I've been thinking about getting a professional songwriter to mentor you girls, and I think I have one lined up. I'm not sure, I need to talk to her directly when I go to Morgan's wine and cheese party tomorrow night at the gallery. But hopefully, I can talk her into it and she can take you girls under her wing. Hopefully she has a lot of good contacts in the music world, so maybe, who knows, you just might be able to snag a recording studio and put something together."

Quinn wasn't real sure about the music world in the age of the Internet, but she was certain that there were plenty of singer-songwriters making independent music that made its way to Spotify or a similar streaming service. How all that worked, Quinn wasn't entirely sure. But she was going to find out from Mia when she talked to her.

At any rate, the girls could certainly get a YouTube channel and try to get their music out to the world that way. Or through TikTok. Again, Quinn wasn't sure about how all that worked, but she was going to find out. She had to give the girls hope of something good on the horizon.

Julia just looked at Quinn with a funny look on her face when Quinn told her about lining up a singer-songwriter to help her and Emerson. And then she burst into tears and ran out of the room.

Emerson shook her head. "Nice going, mom," she said.

"What did I say?" Quinn asked, feeling completely confused.

"What do you think you said?" Emerson asked. "You just told Julia about a way she can get her one dream in life, which is to be a song lyricist."

"Sugar, I don't understand," Quinn said.

"It means there's going to be one more thing that's gonna be ripped away from her when that old bat Hannah gets ahold of her," Emerson said pointedly. "Way to go, mom, giving her one more thing that she's going to miss when she goes to New York City and is forced to become a lawyer."

And then Emerson sarcastically clapped her hands slowly before giving Quinn the stink eye and heading up to her and Julia's room, which was where Julia apparently ran to, sobbing.

Quinn took a deep breath. She was doing so many things wrong. Just handling this situation all wrong. But the thing of it was, she had no idea how to handle this situation right. What was she supposed to say or do to make things at least a little bit better?

Unfortunately, there were no good answers. And she started to think that maybe it wasn't such a good idea to get

Mia involved in the situation, anyhow. Because Emerson was probably right. If Quinn went through with her plan and got Mia to come over to mentor the girls, and then Julia really got into it, it would be that much more devastating when she went to New York City to live with Hannah.

If she went to live with Hannah, Quinn corrected herself. *Not when, if.*

Just then, Sarah finally arrived home. Quinn took one look at her and knew that the news wasn't good. To say the least.

Sarah and Quinn sat down and talked through the night about the whole situation. By the time Quinn and Sarah stopped talking, about midnight that night, Quinn knew one thing.

Julia wasn't exaggerating when she talked about Hannah's controlling nature.

If anything, she was minimizing it.

CHAPTER 9

SARAH

*T*he day after she talked to Mary and Hannah about Julia, Sarah knew it was time to go to war. She was going to hire the best attorney she could find. She asked around to everybody that she knew in town. Unfortunately, most of the people she knew in town were in the same boat she was – they were also new to town, so they didn't necessarily know who would be good in this situation.

But Quinn was going to Morgan's wine and cheese party that evening, and Sarah decided to go along. She called Mary to make sure Mary didn't mind coming over and watching the girls, and she didn't, so Mary was going to come to the house at 7.

Sarah felt a little strange about making sure that the girls had supervision. After all, they were both 13 years old, so they should be old enough to stay by themselves. But Sarah was old-school, and so was Quinn, and both of them thought Julia and Emerson should have adult supervision, especially in the evenings.

Besides, the two girls were on a baking spree and had been for the past couple of days. Considering the appliances in the kitchen were gas appliances, there was always a chance that the two girls could blow up the house if they weren't careful. Of course, Sarah knew that probably wasn't going to happen, but one never knows.

Ava wasn't going to be able to watch the girls because she was busy with the winery that evening. Her daughter Samantha had arrived in Los Angeles, and Samantha was working with Ava and Kayla Brentwood, who was the owner of a local bakery that apparently did a lot of catering and cake baking. Ava told Sarah that she had met with Kayla and Samantha, and the three of them got along famously and had entered into an arrangement where Ava and Sarah's winery would supply the wine for Kayla's catering events and Kayla would supply the food and cakes for Ava and Sarah's winery events. The entire thing was going to benefit everybody, and Ava was really excited about it.

She was also thrilled about the fact that her daughter Samantha was going to be living so close again. Ava was also quite close to her son, but he seemed to have a lot on his mind. Ava had no idea what those things were, but she worried about him. But Samantha was stable, in that she was going for the career she loved and she was really good at it. And, Samantha was going to be a real asset to Sarah and Ava's winery.

So, because Ava couldn't watch the girls that evening, and Sarah was going to the art gallery, Mary was fine with coming over.

Sarah was completely stressed out about the situation, but she didn't let on to the girls. Julia knew what Sarah knew about Hannah, so there was no need to tell Julia about what Mary said about Hannah and her controlling nature. There really wasn't much to say to Julia about what was going on, because Sarah didn't know. She really hoped to find a good attorney who could advise her on the situation. And, at any rate, even if an attorney told Sarah bad news, Sarah knew it was going to be a matter of picking the right judge and making sure that judge was able to see just how destructive Hannah was going to be to Julia's life.

It all came down to the judge. If the wrong judge was assigned to the case, all would be lost. If the judge just looked at blood relation, then that would be all she wrote. But if they could just find a judge able to look at the totality of the circumstances, Sarah might have a chance.

So, it also kind of hinged on the attorney. She had to find an attorney who knew all the judges and how they worked and how they decided custody cases. Because there was one thing Sarah knew about judges, and that was that if they were assigned the wrong judge, they could get out of that judge's courtroom and try to find somebody else. So that was why Sarah really wanted to find somebody who knew each and every judge in the circuit.

Mary came to watch the girls right at seven. They were still baking away. There were endless cookies, brownies, cakes, and pies that were cluttering up the kitchen. They were all keto-friendly, sugar-free and delicious, so Sarah knew she could take at least some of these baked goods over to Morgan's wine and cheese party and they would be a hit. So she packed up several dozen different cookies and brownies in some Tupperware in anticipation of getting rid of them at Morgan's gallery.

Sarah tried a few of the yummy baked goods, and she was so impressed that these baked goods were made by two 13-year-old girls, one of whom, Emerson, ate nothing but junk food up until about a year or so ago when she came to live with Quinn. Sarah's favorite were the white chocolate peppermint Brownies, which were delicious fudge brownies baked with white chocolate peppermint chips.

It was amazing what could be done with sugar-free products these days, Sarah thought. In her day, if you wanted to make something sugar-free yet sweet, you had to squirt some gross syrup made of saccharine into your food or drink or whatever. Nowadays, there was a veritable potpourri of sugar-free options, from Monk Fruit and Erythritol to Stevia, all of which were all-natural and sweeter than sugar.

On the way to the gallery, Sarah and Quinn talked about what was about to happen. And Quinn admitted she was not just going to this wine and cheese thing because she wanted to hang out and drink wine and eat cheese and scrumptious sugar-free Brownies, but that she was going to be seeing an old friend who hopefully would be able to help Julia and Emerson with their songwriting endeavors.

"Oh, tell me about this friend," Sarah said.

And then Quinn told Sarah all about a girl by the name of Mia who Quinn was very close with when she lived in the Bensonhurst area of Brooklyn in the late 80s-early 90s. Quinn's face really lit up when she talked about the woman. And it was obvious that Quinn was really anxious to reconnect with her old friend.

Mia seemed like a really cool person, so Sarah was also looking forward to meeting her. Sarah was always excited to meet new people, and she was really excited about the possibility that she could talk up her winery amongst the gallery guests. She also knew that for future events, Morgan was going to use Sarah and Ava's winery to supply the alcohol. Unfortunately, because the wine and cheese soirée had been planned for several months, Morgan had already contracted with a different winery for the event. But, definitely, Morgan was going to use Sarah and Ava's winery in the future.

Sarah and Quinn arrived at the gallery, and Quinn immediately spied a woman about their age. The woman was average height, but in really good shape for somebody in her mid-50s. She was dressed in a black tank top, a ripped jeans jacket, and faded jeans. Her hair was cut in an asymmetrical style, with one half of her hair buzz cut above the year, with the other half cut to her chin. She was very pretty and youthful, with big blue eyes, high cheekbones, and Angelina Jolie lips. She was holding a glass of wine and talking to some people when Quinn walked up to her.

When Quinn walked up to her, she shrieked so loudly that people probably heard her on the beach, which was about 1/2 an hour away from the downtown gallery. "Oh my God, Quinn Barlowe! How the hell are you doing?"

Quinn and Mia embraced for what seemed like half an hour. But it really was only a few minutes. Sarah walked over to the two and smiled.

It was obvious that the two women had a lot of catching up to do, so, after Quinn introduced Mia and Sarah, Sarah excused herself and went to go and network with other people.

CHAPTER 10

QUINN

*Q*uinn was *so* nervous when she walked into the gallery event. She had the nervous anticipation of somebody who was really anxious to see somebody, but not really knowing how they would be received. It had been so long since she talked to Mia. She had no idea what to expect. Would Mia be a completely different person? Would she not be the same free-spirited fun person she was when Quinn hung out with her back in the day? It was hard to know, of course.

And maybe Mia wasn't anxious to see her. Quinn and Mia had lost touch with one another, and neither woman had bothered to contact the other all these years. Quinn had never received a friend request from Mia on Facebook and Mia had never followed her on Instagram. And Quinn also never sent Mia a friend request on Facebook and she'd never bothered to find out if Mia had an Instagram or Twitter account. In short, Quinn had never really bothered to try to connect with Mia all these years. Maybe there was a reason why the two women hadn't connected for over thirty years.

But, when Quinn saw Mia in the crowded gallery, and

made a beeline for her, it was obvious that she and Mia still had the same connection. Mia was so excited to see Quinn that she gave her a huge hug, and, when the two let go of their embrace, Mia had tears in her eyes.

"Mia, it's so great to see you," Quinn said. And it was. Mia looked absolutely fantastic. It seemed that she didn't age a single day in the 30+ years since Quinn had seen her. It was obvious just by looking at Mia that she still marched to the beat of her own drummer. And that was a very welcome thing for Quinn.

"Hell, it's great to see you too," Mia said. "Man, you look like you just stepped out of a TARDIS. Like you were transported from the early 90s until now, looking exactly the same as you did back then."

Quinn started laughing. "Still a *Doctor Who* fan, huh?"

"Always." And then Mia smiled and laughed again. "Man. I can't tell you many times I've thought about you over the years. Wondering what you're up to, wondering how many men's hearts you'd broken. Wondering if you were still with that loser Benjamin." She started to shake her head. "That dude did not know what he had, trust me."

"The loser Benjamin is long gone, and nobody has taken his place. What about you? How many hearts have you broken along the way?"

"Left a trail from New York to Los Angeles," she said. "Just kidding. Newly single. Turns out lesbians are just as shady and cheaty as straight people. Who knew?" And then she started to laugh.

"You too?" Quinn asked. "That's what happened to the loser Benjamin, by the way. He met a woman at the restaurant who actually really loved wine. And that was that."

"What's that supposed to mean?" Mia asked. "A woman who loves wine. As I can recall, you put back that wine with the best of them. There must've been something else about this woman other than the fact she loved wine."

Quinn was about to explain what she meant when Mia shook her head and put her hand on Quinn's shoulder.

"Oh, I remember now," Mia said. "It's all coming back to me. Your loser husband was constantly getting on your ass because you didn't want to learn everything about wine-making or something like that. Some dude tries to tell me how to appreciate wine, I'd be like 'leave me alone, dude. Let me enjoy my Chardonnay without having to learn how the grapes were pressed.'"

Quinn laughed. "Yeah, the guy was a loser, as it turns out."

Mia rolled her eyes but laughed. "He was?" She pretended to look astonished. "Really? I thought he was a standup dude, even though he was never home, tried to infantilize you and always tried to go out of his way to make you feel like you were 2 inches tall. Trust me, the day he met the other woman was the day somebody up there smiled on you."

"I know. I didn't know it at the time. It's only when I look back when I realize that him leaving me for another woman was the best thing that ever happened to me."

Mia nodded. "Hell yeah it was. It's just like my pit bull dog, Rosie. Got her at a shelter. She was a street dog, a stray. Rosie probably thought when she came to that shelter that she was having a really bad day. You know, that shelter's all crowded and smells terrible, she's getting her stomach sliced open to take out her ovaries or whatever it is they do when they spay a dog. She probably thought that life was a bitch on the day, no pun intended, because she's, you know, a literal bitch. But you know what? I'm sure when she looks back, if dogs can look back, she realizes that the day she was brought into that shelter was her lucky day, because that's where I found her. In that shelter. She lives like a queen now."

Quinn actually followed Mia's story about her dog and

understood what she was getting at. She always was on Mia's wavelength. "So, in the story, I guess I'm Rosie."

"Damn right. Just like Rosie thought her life was in the toilet when she was brought into the shelter, you thought your life was in the toilet when that loser Benjamin left you for another woman. But it was only the beginning of the life you were supposed to lead. Am I right?"

Quinn nodded and laughed. "Oh, you don't know how right you are," she said. "My life's amazing. I have a great career, great friends, and a great daughter."

"Tell me about your daughter," Mia said.

"Oh, how long you got? Actually, my daughter is why I'm here talking to you."

And then Quinn gave Mia the Cliff's Notes version of what happened with Emerson's conception and how much trouble Emerson was at first and how Emerson had blossomed since she came to live with Quinn. And then Quinn told her all about Emerson's knack for writing music and Julia's knack for writing lyrics.

" Dude, that's rough," Mia said when Quinn told her the whole story about being date-raped and conceiving Emerson as a result. "Good on you, though, taking her in like that. You know, it's like Rosie again. What seemed like the worst day of your life came out to be something pretty amazing, sounds like, since your Emerson is so talented and all."

"Yeah, I've come to realize something along my 55 years," Quinn said. "You can never tell if something's going to be a good event or a bad one until you get some space and time. And you're right, at the time when that happened, I was devastated beyond belief. To be raped and pregnant and giving up that child." Quinn shook her head. "And, I'll admit, when Emerson first came to me, I didn't think it would turn out okay. She was a handful, and that's being charitable. But she's calmed down quite a bit and she has her best friend living with her. So, for the moment, at least, she's doing great."

"Her best friend's living with her? Did you take her in, too?"

"No." And then Quinn filled her in about how she decided to live with Sarah who was Julia's stepmother, and about how Sarah might lose custody of Julia because of Hannah filing a custody lawsuit.

"Man," Mia said. "That Hannah sounds like a piece of work. I mean, who does that? Swoop in, try to take a kid away for no good reason, especially if the kid's doing well. I mean, hasn't that poor kid gone through enough with her dad dying? No, apparently that woman wants her pound of flesh for some reason. Sounds like she really hates her sister, because, after all, she'll be taking the kid away from her Aunt Mary, too."

"I know. I don't know what gets into people's heads sometimes. All I know is I don't think Hannah's looking at Julia's best interest at all. Then again, it's entirely possible that she thinks she's doing the right thing. If her mind is twisted enough, she'll believe that."

"No," Mia said, adamantly shaking her head. "Sounds to me like she's got an axe to grind, and she's going to use an innocent 13-year-old as the axe."

"Really? You think Hannah might be as twisted as all that?"

"Oh yes, I forgot that about you. You always want to see the best in people. You were never cynical like me." Then she shrugged. "Then again, I probably need to give people a break once in a while. So, maybe I'm just talking out my tuchus. Anyhow, I really hope Sarah finds a bad-ass lawyer who won't take no crap. That's what you need. A shark. And the right judge."

"Yeah, I think that's what she's going to need," Quinn said. "You know anybody like that?"

"Do I look like I hang with a bunch of lame attorneys?" Mia asked with a raise of her eyebrows and a smile. "Don't answer that question," she joked. "No, unfortunately, I don't know anybody who would be good in this situation. But I see your friend walking around talking to people. She can probably find somebody who knows somebody."

"I hope so, because that's why she's here. Well, that and she wants to network around and pimp out her winery."

"Oh, she has a winery?" Mia said. "'You just can't seem to get away from those wine snobs, can you?" she joked.

" Yeah, maybe it's because I can't seem to get away from the wine, either. Trust me, I still love my mommy juice."

"Mommy juice," Mia said. "You know, all those nights we hung out on your fire escape drinking Boones Farm or shotgunning PBR or Milwaukee's Beast, I never imagined you with a kid. Or me. But, you know, I never had any spawn. God forbid I did. I mean, could you imagine me with a rug rat?"

"Actually, I think you'd be a great mom," Quinn said.

Mia rolled her eyes and smiled. "Oh, yeah, a great mom. 'Sure, kid, you don't have to do your homework. I never did and look at me! I'm singing songs on the street, hoping somebody throws a dollar bill into my guitar case. Don't you want to be just like me?'"

"Oh, come on, you're doing great for yourself."

"I guess. I'm working as a songwriter, at any rate. Notice I don't say the words singer-songwriter, because, it turns out not a whole lot of people wanted to hear me sing after all. Who knew?"

" I don't think you have a view of your own talent," Quinn said. "I seem to remember you filling coffeehouses and people actually put money into your guitar case. I think you're a better singer than you think."

Mia shrugged. "I hold my own, I guess. But it's not like people were signing me up to record labels or even flocking to my YouTube channel when I had it up. I didn't exactly set the world on fire and go viral. But that's okay. I have a knack for writing songs, and that's been good enough for me."

Quinn took a deep breath. She had no idea if Mia would agree to mentor the girls, or even if she did that for people. So she didn't know how her request was going to land. "Do you ever help young songwriters? You know, be like a mentor or anything like that?"

Mia laughed. "Again, I don't want to be a role model for nobody. But, yeah, I think I'd consider mentoring for a couple of young girls if the right woman asked me, and the price is right, of course. Gotta pay my bills somehow."

Quinn smiled. She hoped Mia would say something like that. "Great. So you'll do it?"

"Yeah, of course." She raised her eyebrows. "If it means a chance for me to spend time with you again, just like old times, I'm there. Count me in. Hell, I'd do it for free."

"I'm sure you would, but I plan on paying you your going rate. Which is?"

Mia shrugged. "I don't really know, because I've never done something like this."

" Well, I've done my research on this, and other people who are singer-songwriters who mentor people or do song-writing editing or whatever it is they do, usually charge around $150 dollars an hour. So, since that's the going rate, that's what I'm going to pay you. I hope that's okay."

Mia smiled and whistled. "$150 an hour just for hanging with a couple of young girls and helping them rhyme some-thing with the word strawberry or something, hopefully helping them rhyme it with something that makes sense? Hell, yes. I'll take it."

Quinn smiled. She was really happy Mia made that decision. Because, just like Mia had implied she was looking forward to hanging out with Quinn, Quinn was looking forward to the exact same thing. She was really looking forward to hanging out with Mia again.

She looked at her friend and wondered if Mia ever thought of her romantically. During all those nights they spent together, hanging out, Mia had never implied that she was even attracted to Quinn. Maybe that was because Mia sensed that Quinn wasn't interested in women in that way. Or at least she wasn't at that time. Or maybe it was because Quinn was married. Whatever the reason, Mia just didn't seem to look at her like that.

And she had no idea how she would broach the subject with her.

She found herself with a pit in her stomach. It was all so confusing for her. On the one hand, she was feeling wildly attracted to the woman. And, if she were being honest with herself, she felt the same way back then. Even if she'd buried her feelings about it back then, she'd felt that way. Granted, she never said a word to Mia about her feelings. She was too frightened back then to say anything, and, besides, she was married at that time.

But would she be able to now? After all, Mia was currently single. That's what she said. And she seemed to make a point of saying that to Quinn. So, there was always a possibility that she would be receptive if Quinn said something to her.

Then again, there was always a possibility that she'd turn her down flat. And that was what was causing Quinn's pit in her stomach. She didn't want to go there if she would end up being humiliated. And that's exactly what she would feel like if she made a move and Mia turned her down. Plus, it could harm their friendship.

And there was one thing she knew right at that moment. And that was that she really wanted to keep Mia in her life now. Mia got away once before, when she moved to Los Angeles, and Quinn always missed her. So, she really hoped that nothing happened to come between their friendship now.

Because she didn't think that she could lose Mia's friendship again. Not now that she had more feelings on the line.

Feelings she'd never acknowledged before.

CHAPTER 11

SARAH

*S*arah found a woman at the party who gave her the name and phone number for a good domestic attorney. The man's name was Kevin Anderson, and he'd been working as a domestic attorney for the past 30 years, since he got out of law school.

So, the day after the party, Sarah gave Kevin a call and arranged to meet with him in his office.

She went to his office and explained everything that she needed from him. Kevin was a handsome guy, with salt-and-pepper hair, olive skin, green eyes, and a ready smile. His eyes lit up when he saw Sarah coming in the door, which Sarah tried not to notice. Actually, she was used to that reaction, even though she was past middle-aged.

She was 54 years old, but had kept in shape over the years, with yoga, Pilates, spinning, and a low-carb diet. It wasn't that she was vain, because she wasn't. She really didn't care how she looked. And when she told herself she didn't care how she looked, she meant it. She wasn't one of those people who told themselves that attractiveness wasn't a priority when really it was. No, for Sarah, it was genuine. She was born stunning, and she was bored with it all. Her fitness and diet routine were only because it made her feel good and sleep like a baby, and those were the only reasons she made all that effort to stay healthy.

After Sarah explained to Kevin what the deal was with everything, and he was making careful notes, she asked him what he thought about the case.

"This is a kind of borderline case that I really don't like to speculate as to how it will turn out," Kevin said. "On the one hand, you have a grieving young girl who's settled into her life and is thriving. She's writing poetry, she's writing songs, she has her best friend, she has her religion, she has her aunt. Unfortunately, you don't have any kind of blood relation to her, you were not married to her father for very long, and, in the eyes of the law, you don't have a legal claim to her *per se*. And if you get an old-school judge, he's probably going to prefer a family member take custody of Julia."

Sarah just nodded her head. She was prepared for somebody to give her straight answers, and it seemed that Kevin was doing just that. And, for that, she was really grateful.

"Okay. So, is it a coin flip?"

"No. It's a little bit better than a coin flip for you," Kevin said. "The reason for this is because the judge needs to look at the best interest of the child. And that's the bottom line. The totality of the circumstances in this case point to the best interest for Julia is to stay right where she is – with you. So, that's the good news."

"And the bad news?"

"The bad news is, there are too many judges in this circuit who would never consider you to be Julia's guardian, just because you don't have any legal claim to her under the law. They follow the old-school dictates of placing a child with a close family member after the death of parents, if there is one available. If Max would've had a will designating you as

81

the custodian of the child after he passed away, it'd be a different situation. But, when there isn't a will with the father's wishes clearly spelled out in writing, it's a different story. Generally, old-school courts are going to go ahead and place a child with a close family member in that case."

Sarah took a deep breath. She was afraid of this. She'd done her own research on the Internet, and what Kevin was saying was what she found as well. Courts look to close family members and then close family friends if there are no family members available. In this case, she was neither. Yes, she was married to Max, but only briefly. It was less than two months between them getting married and him dying, and she barely knew Max before she got married to him. So she wouldn't even be considered to be a close family friend, *per se*. At any rate, because there *was* a close family member who wanted custody of Julia, that close family member would get first priority.

"Okay." Sarah didn't know what to say. This whole situation just sucked.

"How come Max didn't write a will designating you as guardian?" Kevin asked.

"Because he died suddenly, really. Before he died, he had a lot going on. He was trying to get everything arranged for his death with dignity plan and there was so much chaos in general moving to California from Massachusetts. He was going to get it all in writing, but he didn't. But he married me. Would the court look at that? I mean, I could testify on the stand that the only reason why he married me was because he wanted a stepmother for Julia. He wanted me to be Julia's mother after he passed."

"Well, that puts you in slightly better stead in the eyes of the court. But only slightly. You know, it probably would've been helpful if he would've at least put something in writing, even in his handwriting, that the reason why he married you was because he wanted a stable guardian for Julia. That would've made a difference. It wouldn't have made all the difference, but it would've been helpful. Like a thumb on the scale. It wouldn't have been dispositive, however."

Sarah sighed. "So, it's going to be an uphill battle?"

"No. Actually, let me qualify that. It will not be an uphill battle if we get the right judge. If we get the wrong judge, it's gonna be like Sisyphus trying to push a boulder up the hill. Not gonna lie. Once I find out who we're assigned, I can certainly tell you more."

"Great. So, Julia's life depends on the whims of the court system."

"Right. Now, bear in mind, since this is a family law case, we can change the judge once if we get the wrong one. You don't have to prove bias or prejudice. You just are automatically entitled to change the judge."

Sarah's ears perked up. She also knew that was the case because she did research, but she wanted to hear it from Kevin, too.

"That sounds promising," Sarah said. "If we draw a bad judge, we can just change him or her to a good one."

Kevin shook his head. "If only it would be as easy as that. My life would be so much better. The problem is, there are a lot of judges who are old-school and rigid. If we're not lucky, and the new judge we're assigned is just as bad or worse than the first judge, then we're stuck unless we can prove bias or prejudice. So, there you are."

"Best-case scenario?" Sarah asked.

"Best-case scenario, we get a judge who I know is going to look at the totality of the circumstances and the best interest of the child and weigh those factors more heavily than the fact that there's blood relation fighting for custody. Worst-case scenario, we get a judge who goes by the book, and automatically wants to award custody to the blood relation. I apply for a change of judge, and I get an even worse one. In that case, it's probably time to settle."

Sarah had no idea what settling would even mean in this case. If Hannah won the case, she'd be taking Julia to New York City, across the country. It wouldn't be like they could share custody, except for maybe allowing Sarah to have custody during breaks, or something like that. But the damage would be done. Julia would be a changed person. She'd be whipped into submission by the controlling Hannah, and Sarah would have very little influence.

"Settle?" Sarah asked. She hated the idea of settling. In her mind, she was going to go for broke, no matter what. Since settling would mean devastation for Julia, she'd much rather take the case to trial, no matter what, because at least she'd have a small chance of prevailing, even if the chance was very small if she got the wrong judge.

"Yes, settle," Kevin said. "Like it or not, most cases settle. Usually, nobody's happy with the terms of the settlement, but that means the settlement was probably just. After all, if one party is completely happy and the other party is completely miserable, it means that the settlement was lopsided. And probably not one that I would advise my client to accept."

Sarah shook her head. "Not doing it. You have to understand, if the settlement dictates that Hannah will get primary custody of Julia, and I only get to see her over winter, spring and summer breaks, or something like that, that would be devastating for that young girl. I'd rather just fight it all the way. Throw everything out on the field, no matter who's the referee. I don't think I can give Hannah an inch."

Kevin grimaced. "I thought you'd say that. No offense, but people always say that in these situations. So it's up to me to give you the reality, as I see it, as soon as we find out who the judge is going to be. I mean, if we get the exact wrong judge for this, and trust me, I know every judge and how they rule,

I'm going to strongly advise you to settle. You're required to go through mediation, and the mediator can help you settle the case. You have to understand, there's not a jury involved with this. It's only the judge making the decision. If you could try the case before a jury, it's a crap shoot, even if the judge is a traditional judge who will always look at the blood relation before a relative stranger. But if it's just the judge, then you have to look at the reality of how that judge is going to rule."

Sarah wasn't liking the sound of this. She couldn't believe that the life of a 13-year-old girl was going to hinge on just one person. That it was going to be like playing roulette. Sarah just had to hope that somehow, someway, the roulette ball landed on the right number. If it didn't, if it skipped over the right number and went to the wrong one, all would be lost. Julia's life would be forever altered, and not for the good.

It seemed so unfair. Sarah wanted Julia to thrive by doing things she loved. Writing poetry and songs, baking, getting involved in causes, and observing her faith in the way that she chose, not observing her faith according to someone else's wishes. Sarah was going to do everything she could to support Julia and her dreams. She wasn't going to, in any way shape or form, try to throw cold water on Julia's passion and fire for the things she loved.

Hannah, on the other hand, if Mary was to be believed, was going to do the opposite. She was going to force Julia onto a very narrow path, and she was just going to quench her spirit.

Julia had such potential to be successful in any number of fields. She could become a songwriter, like Quinn's friend Mia. Or maybe she could follow her passion for baking into becoming a pastry chef or a cake decorator, just like Ava's daughter Samantha. Or maybe she could become an activist, as she also had a passion for causes like climate change, women's rights, and things like that. She could become the next Greta Thunberg, the young girl who was so passionate about climate change issues that she became a worldwide phenomenon. After all, Greta Thunberg started her climate change activism at the age of 15, so she could see Julia and Emerson doing something similar, but on a smaller scale, when they got just a little bit older.

Julia could go either way. She could either be made into an automaton, going down the road that Hannah set for her, and not deviating because Hannah wouldn't let her deviate, or she could become the woman that she was supposed to become. And her entire life was going to hinge on the whims of one person – the judge.

Sara looked down at Kevin's desk. And then she looked at his box of Kleenex, and wondered if she was going to have to use them. After all, she was about to burst into tears. She couldn't help it. It was such a sense of injustice to know that Julia's fate was going to rely on a coin flip.

Kevin saw Sarah eyeing his box of Kleenex and he gently pushed the Kleenex a little bit closer to her. Sarah smiled at the gesture. Obviously, Kevin was a man who was a bit sensitive to nonverbal cues, which was a good sign. In Sarah's experience, many men were not so sensitive to these cues, or they just didn't care to notice.

Sarah nodded, and took one of the Kleenexes and dabbed her eyes. "Thank you for putting it to me straight. But, like I said, even if I get the most hard-ass judge in the circuit, I want to fight. It's just too important. Even if there's just even a 2% chance that I could win the case, I'm going to take that chance. Because the alternative is just too bleak for that poor girl."

Kevin looked at Sarah solemnly and nodded his head. "That bad, huh?"

Sarah nodded. "That bad. I mean, there's not abuse or anything like that. Unless you consider trying to control every aspect of someone's life abuse."

Kevin laughed. "If a parent trying to control every aspects of a child's life is considered to be abuse, then abuse would be considered endemic. Unfortunately, that seems to be the nature of a lot of people. And usually it backfires, but you can't tell anybody that."

Sarah thought about her own mother. Colleen was certainly somebody who knew her own mind and never wanted to take anybody's views into account but her own. But, to her credit, Colleen never tried to dictate to Sarah or Ava what they were going to do in life. Sarah made a huge mistake when she decided to follow Nolan, her billionaire ex-boyfriend, around the world instead of pursuing her chosen career in architecture. But Colleen never tried to do anything to dissuade her from that idea. Basically, Colleen was the kind of mother who allowed her children to make their own mistakes and learn from them. Which Sarah did, even if it took her a long time to get out of that situation.

"Well, I'm going to go ahead and hire you," Sarah said. "I guess we're going to throw the dice and hope for the best. There's nothing else we can really do."

Kevin took a deep breath. "No, you're right. With any luck, we'll get an open-minded judge. There are several of them in the circuit. Good judges who take all the evidence into account, who listen to the child, especially if the child is older, like Julia is at the age of 13. Who actually look at the best interest of the child. If we get one of them, I'd say our chances are quite good."

Sarah dabbed her eyes again. She was determined not to cry, at least until she got out into the hallway. "Give me the percentages."

"Well, it's kind of a sliding scale. There are certain judges in the circuit that if we happen to get lucky and draw them, your chances are probably 90%. And then there are certain judges in the circuit where it's more a 50-50 chance. And then at the bottom of it, if you get the absolute worst judge, and by worst judge I mean somebody who is close-minded to any factor but blood relation, you're probably looking at 2%."

"2% ain't zero," Sarah said. "We fight, no matter what. Okay?"

"Okay. It's helpful for me to know what the client expects right up front. But, like I said, most of my clients come in here and say fight fight fight. But then when the reality hits, they end up settling. Not that that's going to be you, but I'm just telling you what my experience has been with people in difficult custody cases."

Sarah didn't say anything but just whipped out her check-book and wrote a fat check for his retainer – $10,000. She handed it to him, and he nodded. "Okay. I guess it's time to go to war. I'll start my investigation today. With any luck, I'll find out that Hannah is secretly a serial killer and I can prove it." And then he smiled. "Sorry, gallows humor. It helps in this profession."

Sarah had to laugh at Kevin's little joke. "Yeah. Maybe you'll get into the investigation find out that Hannah is giving Jeffrey Dahmer a run for his money."

"Even so, there are some judges in this circuit who'll give Hannah custody even if she is a serial killer. No joke."

"Great. That's good to know. What's wrong with people?"

"It's just that there are certain judges who follow the letter of the law," he said. "They look at the guidelines, which specify that blood relations are preferred, and that's all they see. By the way, it was a slight exaggeration when I said there are certain judges who'd award custody to a serial killer blood relation over a loving non-blood relation. But it's only a slight exaggeration. At any rate, I'll get to work. I'll know more when I find out what judge we have."

As Sarah left his office and took the elevator down, she had to hold onto the elevator rails to keep herself from falling. She still couldn't believe that the life of a young girl was going to depend on the cruel fate of the justice system. She was brought back to her own court case so many years ago, when she was forced to plead guilty to a felony she didn't commit, because there was just too much of a chance that she would lose her case in court. That was obviously an injustice that changed her entire life. Her path would've been so much different if that incident didn't happen.

And now, the fate of Julia seemed to be just as capricious as Sarah's own fate. It was going to be the flip of a coin, the turn of a roulette wheel, the roll of the dice. Pick your cliché.

And if the dice turned up snake eyes, Julia was toast.

And that seemed so unfair.

CHAPTER 12

QUINN

Quinn was *so* excited for the girls to meet Mia. She was really worrying a lot about both Emerson and Julia these days. Julia was getting more and more depressed, which actually made her more productive. She wasn't baking so much anymore, but she was writing a lot of poetry and songs.

And she told Quinn that she was sorry for her reaction when Quinn told her about finding a songwriting mentor for her.

"When you first told me about it, I reacted so wrong," Julia had said to Quinn. "I know that this is you doing something very nice for me, and, when I thought about it, I realized it'll be a great thing." And then she paused for a long time, her eyes cast down to the floor. "And even if I can't use this mentor in the long term, because I'm going to be moving across the country with my Aunt Hannah, Emerson can benefit."

Quinn's heart went out to the poor girl. Her life was up in the air, to say the very least. After Sarah had seen her new lawyer, she told Quinn all about what Kevin had told her. It didn't sound good, at least if the wrong judge was chosen.

"Well, sugar, I understand," Quinn said. "And I'm not going to try to tell you that you're not going to end up living with Hannah. I am going to tell you that you are a very talented songwriter, and, with Mia's help, you can become even better. And here's something to consider. Even if the worst thing happens, and you end up living with Hannah, you'll be 18 in five years. You can choose your own life at that point, and your songwriting ability will never leave you. So, no matter what, you're going to be able to benefit from Mia's guidance."

"I guess."

Julia seemed doubtful about the prospect of getting out from under Hannah's iron grip. And Quinn knew why. Women like Hannah could be devastating to a young mind and spirit. While Quinn rationally thought that Julia could continue her chosen path after emancipating herself from Hannah, she knew that the reality was probably different. Julia was such a sensitive soul that she would be very impressionable. She was malleable. If she was more like Emerson, who was so strong-willed that nobody could tell her what to do, Quinn would've been more hopeful for Julia's future. But Julia wasn't like Emerson, so Quinn was quite worried.

So, Mia came over to the house to meet Emerson and Julia a couple of days after Quinn and Mia reconnected at Morgan's wine and cheese party. Emerson and Julia took one look at the youthful-looking Mia, with her asymmetrical hair, long black T-shirt dress that was formfitting and sleeveless, and combat boots, and it was obvious that both girls took an immediate liking to her.

Quinn smiled. Mia just had a positive, effervescent energy that was so attractive. Mia was the kind of person who people just automatically liked when they saw her.

Apparently, by the look on Emerson and Julia's face, they were no different. They really liked her the second they saw her.

"Okay, so you two girls are my new victims," Mia said with a smile. "Let's hear what you got."

So, the gang moved to the piano room. That was what Quinn was calling the sunroom, which now sported the baby grand that Ava had bought for Emerson. Emerson sat down at the piano, and Julia started to sing one of their songs. Mia listened to them for a couple of bars before she stopped them and made some suggestions for the lyrics and the tempo.

"I see what you guys are going for, kind of a Tori Amos meets Sarah Bareilles vibe. I like it. However, I think the tempo is a little bit too fast on the bridge. But the bridge is very good, by the way. So, your lyrics are metaphorical and symbolic. Let me just help you shape some of your metaphors."

So, for a couple of hours, Mia helped Julia sharpen her lyrics so they were more pinpointed as to what she wanted to say in the song, and she stood behind Emerson as she played the piano and made suggestions on tempos and cords.

Quinn sat in the piano room at first, watching the action unfold, but then she had other things to do – namely, her job. She was working on a project for a London flat, and she'd just received the pictures and the dimensions for this particular flat, so it was time to get to work on it.

She was working hard on the project, sending her client a list of artwork and furniture and flooring to buy, when Mia came into the room. "Hey. What's going on?"

"Just working. How are things?"

"Great. Those two girls are really talented. And they were a joy to work with. Believe me, that's a relief. As I said, I've never done this kind of thing before, but I know people don't always take criticism well. Even constructive criticism. So, I admit, I was biting my nails before I came over here. But, they did really well with my two cents."

"Well, I can assure you that your advice to the girls is worth much more than two cents. Exactly worth $150 an hour," Quinn said with a laugh. "Thank you again for coming over and doing this."

"Oh my God, thank you for thinking of me." Then Mia sat down on the leather seat next to Quinn's workspace. "How much more work do you have to do?" she asked her.

"A couple of hours. I'm going to quit a little early today." Then Quinn raised an eyebrow. "Why? You free tonight?"

Mia shrugged. "Yeah, I am. Why? You got something in mind?"

"I do. I mean, we can't go out to eat or anything like that. Sarah and Ava are both at their winery, so I need to stay home and watch the girls, but maybe you can come over and we could grill something and go down to the beach."

That was something Quinn loved to do. Ava's house, which was where Quinn, Sarah, Julia, and Emerson were staying for the time being while their own house on Venice Beach was being renovated, had a beautiful deck that went right up to the beach.

"Sounds like a plan. I'll come back with some mommy juice. What do you say, around seven?"

"Sounds good." Quinn felt her heart racing. Fluttering. It was weird. She hadn't really felt that way about anybody. Ever. Well, maybe she felt that way about Benjamin at the time. It was hard to say, because the bitterness she still felt towards him all these years clouded her judgment. Was she ever in love with him? She was sure she was back then, otherwise she wouldn't have married him and followed him to New York.

Would she have? Maybe. She was so young when she married him. It was a lifetime ago at this rate. So, it was hard to know at this point, almost 30 years later, how she felt back then. But, what she knew was she hadn't had a man in her life ever since Benjamin left her in the lurch. And as she looked into Mia's eyes, which were so clear blue they were piercing, she wondered if the reason why she didn't date men all these years was because maybe she just didn't want to date men. Maybe she liked women all along. It was possible. Although Quinn knew she wasn't attracted to any women along the way, either. For almost 30 years, she had no desire to be with anybody.

Was that about the change?

CHAPTER 13

QUINN

That evening, Mia came over for dinner. Quinn fixed a nice salmon on the grill, and, because Emerson was also eating dinner with them, she had to make something vegan. So, she had grilled a Beyond Burger topped with cashew cheese and served it with a salad on the side for her daughter.

As she watched Emerson eagerly dig into the burger and the salad, she marveled again about how far Emerson had come since the day she came to her door. At that time, Emerson wouldn't eat a vegetable if her life depended on it. She acted like she was allergic to anything not packaged and processed. Now, here she was, digging into her salad of butter lettuce, avocado, tomato, olives, and cashew goat cheese. And she really loved the Beyond Burger.

Julia hadn't yet joined Emerson in the vegan thing, so she ate the salmon with the adults. Quinn thought it was only a matter of time for Julia to join Emerson in veganism, as her daughter and her best friend were like two peas in a pod in a lot of ways. Quinn just couldn't imagine the two of them ever being separated.

It was such a nice evening. It was just the four of them, sitting on the enormous deck that was in the back of Ava's new home in Malibu, and they could hear and see the waves rolling in. The only thing was, the sun didn't set over the ocean right there, but, rather, it sat behind the hills. Quinn had heard stories from locals about the flash of green light that would happen right when the sun sets. She hadn't yet seen the green light, but she wanted to, because she wanted to know if it was true. She was just very curious about that.

The dogs were joining them on the deck, of course. Sarah's dog, Bella, who was a pit bull mix, sat at Quinn's feet, begging. Kona, who was Quinn's dog, and was a shepherd-pug mix, was also begging from Quinn. Of course the two dogs would be begging from Quinn, because she was a soft touch when it came to feeding them from the table. She knew she shouldn't. Her vet told her not to. Yet, she could never resist the lure of the big brown eyes and soft wet noses.

As Quinn sat there and fed the dogs from the table, little by little, Mia laughed. "I always knew you'd be like this with a dog, even back in the day when you didn't have a dog, because where would you have put a dog in that little tiny apartment of yours in Bensonhurst?"

Quinn smiled. "How did you know I would be like this with a dog?" Quinn lightly rubbed Bella's ears and bent down to kiss the top of Kona's head. She absolutely loved these canines. As in, if there was some kind of an emergency evacuation, she'd stay with the dogs at the house if she couldn't find a shelter that would take them. She used to think that people who would ride out hurricanes were absolute idiots, until she found out that a lot of the people who ride out the storms did so because they were protecting their pets. And Quinn could see that.

And, there was always a chance that they would have an

emergency evacuation there in Los Angeles. There were three things to look out for in Los Angeles – earthquakes, mudslides, and wildfires. The earthquakes, thank goodness, were not much of a problem. Tremors happened quite a bit, or at least that was what Quinn heard from the locals, but actual earthquakes that level buildings and kill people hadn't happened in the Los Angeles area for many years. The last big one was in the San Fernando Valley in 1971. It killed 65 people and injured 2000 and caused millions in property damage. Before that, you'd have to go all the way back to 1933, where 115 people were killed in Long Beach. She used to hear, when she was a kid, that California would one day break off from the mainland and sink into the ocean, but Quinn saw little chance of that happening. Maybe one day, billions of years into the future, but not right now.

Destructive earthquakes rarely happened, but mudslides and wildfires? Those happened all the time. They damaged homes, killed people, and mudslides were known to carry away cars and collapse houses. But Quinn knew that in the event of a mudslide or a wildfire, she would protect her pets, who she referred to as her babies. They were just too precious not to.

"I knew you'd be a soft touch with a pupper because that's just how you were. Let me guess – you spend far too much time online looking at funny pet videos when you should be working. How close am I?"

Quinn thought about that very day. She got sucked into a series of videos about funny pets who don't want to go to the vet, and spent the better part of an hour watching it. Then she found a YouTube channel about a couple of guys in Australia who pick dogs up in their van and let them run around their massive estate all day, and watched that for another hour when she should've been working.

"Guilty as charged," Quinn said. "Sometimes it's just stress reducing. You know, you've had a bad day or something like that, and just seeing those fur babies on screen makes you smile and laugh."

Mia had a bottle of beer that she was sipping on, and she took a swig of it. "You're lucky you have a beach for your puppers to run on. I live in a loft, in the middle of a concrete jungle, and I feel for my Rosie sometimes. I'd love for her to have more room to roam, but I just have to settle for taking her to one of the off-leash dog beaches."

Quinn smiled. "You live in a loft? Where at?"

"My building is in a renovated toy factory in the arts district. It's called, appropriately enough, the Toy Factory lofts. It's like a block away from Morgan's gallery. You should come over. I think you'll like it. I think even with your interior decorator eye, you'll be impressed."

Of course Mia lived in a loft. Quinn couldn't imagine her living anywhere else but in a loft. "Is that an invitation?"

"Hell, yeah. I mean, it's not like you're going to come to my loft and be able to sit on a deck and hear the waves coming in or nothing like that. But my place has its own charm and I love living in the Arts District. Because you know I have a lot of friends in the art community. Including Morgan. She's a really cool person, that Morgan. And I love her wife, too. Emma Claire."

"It'll be like old times if I come over," Quinn said wistfully. "Your place have a fire escape that we could sit on and drink Boones Farm or PBR?"

Quinn thought it would be so much fun to recreate the old days. Oh, to be that 22-year-old again, who doesn't have a care in the world except for an absent husband and a crime-filled neighborhood, but who thought the future would be her oyster. And, in a way, she was living in that oyster she had envisioned for herself back then. The only problem was she now was over 30 years older and now had a lot of bad memories that hadn't happened back then. But a part of her would've loved to have gone back to that young girl who was so naïve and innocent.

Then again, if she was given the chance to live her life all over again, on the condition that she would have to live her life over again exactly the way that she lived it the first time, she wouldn't. Not a chance in hell. The only way that she'd ever be willing to live her life over would be if she could fix the mistakes she made along the way. But that would mean that Emerson would not have been born, because obviously Quinn wouldn't want to live *that* part of her life over again. So it was a good thing that she could never have the chance for a total rewind.

Anyhow, she was happy with her life right at that moment. She was fulfilled in her career, she had a great daughter and great friends, and now she had her old friend back in her life. Life could not be better. Why would she want to go back to those days if she didn't have to?

"Alas, no," Mia said. "My loft building doesn't have fire escapes. But it does have a doorman, landscaped gardens, a sun deck, and a pool on the roof. I know, I know, you didn't think I'd be so fancy. That's okay, I never thought I'd be so fancy, either. But, that's me now. Just call me fancy Mia."

"Oh, that's okay," Quinn said. "We'll just have to make do. Besides, I really didn't want to pick up a bottle of Boone's Farm, anyhow. Even though, back in those days, I loved that stuff. Yeah, we only drank it because it was cheap, and boy did it give me a hangover. But it was really tasty, too. It was sweet and fruity, and I could drink it all day."

Mia took a sip of her beer and held it out for Quinn to clink her beer with it. Quinn smiled and clinked her beer against Mia's beer.

The girls had been playing with the dogs, and they were both ready to go in and call it a night. Quinn knew that

Emerson still enjoyed playing Fortnite online, which she probably would do in the computer room when she went into the house. Julia was probably going to go into their room and write some poems or read some epic fantasy novel that she was so into these days. It seemed that most of Julia's novels she read involved some kind of a white queen in a magical land. She really loved those novels, and she explained that they were escapist.

"Quinn," Julia had said when Quinn asked her what appealed about these fantasy books. "I've had such a bad year, with my dad dying and my old witch of an aunt trying to get me. Sometimes I just want to get away to a place where none of that exists, and that's what I do when I read these novels. I escape into a place that doesn't exist and can't exist. I just don't want to read anything that resembles the world we live in."

Quinn said she could relate to the desire to escape to a different place. She really wished that she could escape to a different place, too, sometimes. But only sometimes.

The girls left to do their things in the house, and Quinn and Mia sat on the deck, drinking their beers and listening to the waves. Mia was suddenly quiet, and it looked like she was lost in thought as she watched the ocean come in.

"What's on your mind?" Quinn asked.

"Nothing much. I was just thinking of that weekend we managed to sneak off and go to Long Island." And then she scrunched up her eyebrows and looked off into the distance. "No, I'm sorry. It was the Rockaways in Queens. We had a crappy old camper that I managed to borrow from my brother, and we parked that camper by the beach and hung out. Do you remember that?" Mia asked.

Of course Quinn remembered that weekend. The two of them got completely schnockered, and Mia flashed her breasts to a couple of guys who asked her to. The guys promised her $50 if she would do it, but, of course, they didn't pay up. They just walked away laughing about how they just got to see a pair of random breasts. But Mia didn't care that they Welched on her. She just thought it was funny, and so did Quinn. And Quinn had no idea why the guys would've laughed at seeing Mia's rack, because her girls were righteous. They were small and firm and rounded. In fact, Quinn admired Mia's body back then, and she admired her body now.

That weekend was epic. Benjamin had a work trip that weekend to a winery in upstate New York. Of course, he was probably banging his girlfriend Karen that weekend, even though Quinn had no idea that was going on. And, to think, Quinn really tried to be good that weekend. The women went out on the town, and, at that time, Mia apparently liked men and women equally. Mia ended up making out with some guy in some bar, and Quinn sat drinking Milwaukee's Best in the corner and tried to fend off various men who try to hit on her because, after all, she was a woman alone in a bar drinking Milwaukee's Best. Everybody probably thought she was easy.

Of course, she wasn't easy. She was anything but easy because she was married and that ring on her finger and the vows she took with Benjamin meant something to her. It meant she couldn't even look at anybody else, because if she looked, she might touch. And she couldn't do that to Benjamin. Now, of course, she knew that Benjamin was doing that to her the whole time he was going on his "work trips" to the wineries in upstate New York.

During the day, the two of them got crisp and red as a couple of lobsters, because they laid out in the sun without an umbrella or any sunscreen. During those times, that's what you did – you put baby oil on instead of sunscreen, even when you were fair, as Quinn and Mia were and are.

Mia pretended to drown because she wanted to meet a cute lifeguard, who happened to be a woman. Unfortunately for Mia, the woman wasn't the one who rescued her, but some brawny dude Mia couldn't care less about - Mia liked men back in the day but she didn't love the muscle heads. Her kind of guy was more of a tattooed dude who loved The Clash and The Ramones and The Pixies. In fact, Quinn remembered that Mia had a requirement back then that any guy that she looked at had to have at least one tattoo and at least one vinyl record by The Clash. Not a lame cassette, but a vinyl record. If the guy had none of those things, he'd officially be too lame for Mia.

"Yeah, I can still see the look on your face when you flashed those two guys," Quinn said. "And I can still see the look on their face when you did that. And you know, I'd bet one hundred dollars that your girls are just as nice today as they were back then. You've really kept yourself well-preserved."

"Ha, ha," Mia said with a roll of her eyes. "Thank you, but I'm 55, just like you. It's not so easy to stay in shape, but I still hit the gym and lift weights and ride those stupid spin bikes. I hate it, but I gotta do it."

Quinn laughed. "I'm sure you look amazing still. Anyhow, do you remember that guy you made out with at the bar?"

"I do. He wasn't that good of a kisser. You know, he kinda slobbered, which is the worst. So, even though he had every vinyl record The Ramones ever produced and he had not just one tattoo sleeve but two, and those tattoo sleeves were epic, let me tell you, no way was I going to let him into Wonderland."

Quinn took a sip of her beer and continued to watch the waves come in. "You mentioned something about being single because women were just as shady as men or something like that. So, do you still like men?"

Mia just shrugged. "I like people. I fall in love with a person, not a gender. I know, that sounds like a big old cliché, but it's true. At least, for me it's true."

"So, do you happen to have anybody in mind?"

Mia smile. " Yeah. But I don't think they're interested."

"They?" Quinn said in a teasing voice. "There's more than one person? Are you thinking about becoming part of a throuple?"

At that, Mia just started laughing. "You know, I had a throuple offer as a matter of fact. Can't say I wasn't tempted, but, no, it's not for me. I'm definitely a one person person. I just said the word they, because I don't want to reveal if it's a man or woman I'm interested in. I don't want to give anything away."

Quinn wondered why Mia was being so mysterious about it all. Mia had an interest, which Quinn really didn't want to hear. Quinn wanted to feel things out and see if Mia felt the same way about her as she felt about Mia. But, apparently, Mia was already looking in a different direction.

"What about you? Any dude catching your eye these days?" Mia asked.

Quinn shook her head. "Back on Nantucket, there was a man who really liked me a lot. He was the guy who worked on Emerson's adoption. He was a really nice guy, very successful, but, I don't know, I just wasn't feeling it."

Mia smiled and took a swig of her beer. "Now, now. You're a real hottie. Like a total smoke show. I'm pretty sure this guy on Nantucket wasn't the only one who tried to become your next squeeze."

Quinn didn't argue with that. She was hit on by quite a few men and asked out many times over the years. She shut them all down. It was just that Asher, her adoption attorney, came the closest to Quinn giving him a chance. Closer than anybody else over the years, at any rate. As for Mia's compliments about her being a hottie and smoke show, she was flattered, but she never saw herself that way.

"Yeah, I guess guys have asked me out over the years. But, I don't know, I just think Benjamin soured me for life on men."

Mia fingered the neck of her beer bottle as she watched the ocean rage. It seemed to be high tide, because several of the waves came all the way up to the barrier that protected the deck from the water. "So," she finally said after a few minutes of looking at the surf and not saying anything. "Your life has been soured on men. You ever think about maybe becoming one of those late-in-life lesbians like Cynthia Nixon, or Catherine Bell or Maria Bello?"

"Don't forget Kelly McGillis," Quinn said. "Charlie Blackwood herself."

"Right," Mia said with a laugh. "I did forget about Kelly McGillis. How could I forget about her? I love *Top Gun.*"

Quinn still wasn't really quite ready to go there. It was still so weird for her. When she was young, she never thought about girls or women romantically. Her first crush was on the Professor on *Gilligan's Island.* And then she had a crush on Warren Beatty, Orioles pitcher Jim Palmer, Eric from the Bay City Rollers, and Paul McCartney. Paul McCartney wasn't really from her era, because he was much older, but her father had the *Revolver* album and she fell in love with his voice. And then she caught *The Yellow Submarine* on television one day and got to see him, and she immediately fell in love. And when she got to be a little bit older, she had a big crush on Sting from *The Police,* which was the first band she ever saw live during their *Synchronicity* tour.

Those were the celebrity crushes she experienced when she was young. And when she was young, she also had crushes on boys her age. There was the boy who was part of her carpool who gave her a Barbie doll for her sixth birthday.

And then there was the boy who, when they played *Farmer in the Dell* in school, chose her as the wife when he was the farmer (The farmer takes the wife, the wife takes the child, the child takes the nurse, etc.). And so it went throughout her school years. She had 100 million crushes along the way, all of them on members of the opposite sex.

So, here she was, 55 years old, after never having any romantic feelings for a member of the opposite sex, and she was having her first-ever crush on a woman. And, as much as she wanted to tell Mia how she was feeling, something was stopping her. She just couldn't get herself to say the words to Mia that she was experiencing a mad crush on her.

"No, I've never thought about it. I don't know, I'm probably just going to be celibate for the rest of my life."

Damn. Why was she being so cowardly? As she looked into Mia's eyes, the only thing she could think of was that she was feeling romantic feelings she hadn't felt in a long time.

Was it true that you could just fall in love with the person and not the gender?

Mia just nodded her head and smiled. "Giving up on love. Well, to each her own. Me, I'm a hopeless romantic. I just know the person I'm supposed to be with is around the corner. One of these days, all those corny love songs I'm so good at writing for other people is going to come true for me. But, you do you." Then she winked. "It's too bad, too. Because you know I probably have a woman I could introduce you to if you wanted."

Quinn knitted her brows. So, Mia was just asking her about becoming a late-in-life lesbian because she wanted to introduce her to somebody. She was sorely disappointed, because she imagined that Mia was asking because she herself was interested.

"Sorry to disappoint. Anyhow, who are you working for

these days with your songwriting?" Quinn was eager to change the subject, because the subject was making her just too uncomfortable. She really wanted to tell Mia how she felt, but apparently Mia didn't feel the same way about her as she felt about Mia. She felt hurt and embarrassed even though she really had nothing to be embarrassed about because she didn't say what was on her mind. So, it was time to get the subject on something that was much more neutral.

Mia gave her a list of names of singers and groups, some of which Quinn knew about because they were very popular and some of which were more independent artists that Quinn had never heard of. But it sounded like Mia was a quite successful songwriter, and Quinn was very proud of her.

While Quinn was proud of her friend, it still stung that Mia wanted to set her up with somebody else.

And she was embarrassed that this still stung.

CHAPTER 14

SARAH

*S*arah was working hard at the winery, along with Ava. She really wanted to take her mind off the whole Julia situation, and working at the winery helped with that. The wines were ready to send out for distribution, and the grapes were ripe for picking. So, every day, Sarah went to the winery and picked grapes and put them into the processing vats along with the different notes that each one would have that would make them unique and special.

Ava and Sarah were getting ready for a catering event that Kayla Brentwood's Sweet Fantasy Bakery and Catering was holding in an exclusive Malibu beach house. It was a charity fundraiser benefiting an environmental group, and there was the possibility that some celebrities would be there. There were rumors that some of the Kardashians would be there, maybe some people from the *Real Housewives* show. When Samantha heard those rumors, she got really excited, because she watched a lot of reality television.

For Sarah, however, she presently didn't watch any kind of reality TV, so she couldn't care less. For her, the Kardashians were simply people who were famous for being famous, nothing more and nothing less, and that just didn't impress her. As for the Real Housewives, they were even less impressive. She'd never seen the show, but she always seemed to read about them in the tabloids when she was in line at the supermarket. It seemed they just were famous for being outrageous back stabbers. Somebody turned over a table in a rage and somebody else, it might've been the same table-turner, went to prison for tax evasion. That was about all she knew about the real housewives, and it was enough. If Sarah lived to be 100, she would never understand the appeal of these shows.

Not that she was opposed to all reality television. She watched *Survivor* back in the day, along with everybody else in the world it seemed like and, she had to admit, she was hooked on *The Bachelor* and *The Bachelorette* for many years. But that was just because she was a romantic who believed that true love could be found over a six week or so period where the lead dated, kissed, and had sex with many different people. She was always shocked, shocked, when the bachelor and bachelorette couples broke up. Eventually, the franchise started choosing leads who were obviously fame-whores and not in it for the right reasons, and that's when Sarah finally weaned herself off that franchise. But it had a good run on Sarah's DVR for a while.

Nevertheless, just the mere fact that the Kardashians were rumored to be at this party meant it was going to be an exclusive affair indeed. And they would be drinking wines from Sarah and Ava's winery. How exciting! And, if she didn't have this whole Sword of Damocles Julia situation hanging over her head, she'd be having the time of her life.

As it was, however, the Julia situation was on her mind constantly. While she was outside harvesting grapes, she was thinking about it. When she was inside processing the grapes, she was thinking about it. When she was inside bottling the wine, she was thinking about it.

She was just happy that she didn't have Ava's job, which was the business side of the winery. Ava was the one who did the marketing, wrote out the contracts, maintained the website, and did the accounting for the business. Sarah didn't think she'd be able to work a job where she had to use her brain, like Ava had to with all her job duties. Ordinarily, Sarah could do such tasks, but not now. At this time, she needed the monotony of harvesting grapes, processing them, and bottling wine. It was rote work, very monotonous, but she needed it. She really needed to just put one foot in front of the other as she walked along the vines, a big straw hat on her head, gloves on her hands, the dirt beneath her feet. She was wielding a large sheath that she used to cut the grapes off the vines in bunches, and then she threw them into a large basket.

Her mind went to that knife, again and again. Oh, if Hannah were there while Sarah had that knife in her hand....Sarah had such dark fantasies that were just not like her.

While she was out in the field, Ava found her to tell her it was time to take a break. "You need to eat," she said. "Come on in."

Sarah shook her head. "No, I need to be out here in the sun. There's lots of vitamin D in sunlight, you know. And vitamin D helps with depression, and that's what I'm trying to stave off."

Sarah usually wasn't one who was prone to depression, but she found that was changing at this time. Probably it had something to do with the fact that she wasn't sleeping very well these days. She'd fall asleep fine, but she would get up at two or three in the morning and not be able to get back to sleep. No matter how hard she tried, she couldn't get back into a slumber, so she usually found herself going out into the living room and watching television or reading a book which was definitely better than tossing and turning and staring at the clock.

Ava had caught her a couple of times in front of the television at three in the morning, when she would come out and use the bathroom and would find Sarah sitting in front of the TV watching some DVR'd show like *The Voice* or some other kind of mindless show. Ava would always ask Sarah what she was doing up at that time, and Sarah would simply answer that she couldn't sleep.

She knew Ava was worried about her, especially because, as was her wont, in addition to her insomnia, she lost her appetite. Whenever she was under a lot of stress, she quit eating. And she had lost 10 pounds just since she talked to Kevin and Kevin told her there was a good chance she would lose custody of Julia. He hadn't yet called her to tell her what judge had been assigned to the case, because, to her knowledge, no judge had been assigned just yet. But that was going to come at any day.

"Sarah, you really need to take a break and have some food. I know you probably don't want something heavy, because heavy food is really hard to eat when you don't feel like eating at all, but I have a nice salad for you with all the things you love. Olives, artichoke hearts, Manchego cheese, sun-dried tomatoes, butter lettuce, and your favorite salad dressing." Ava had her hands on her hips, which told Sarah that she was losing patience with her. Ava was, for the past few days, trying to tempt Sarah with all her favorite foods, but Sarah would always say she wasn't hungry and to leave her alone.

Now, apparently, Ava wasn't going to take no for an answer.

Sarah finally just took a deep breath, and took off her

gloves and hat. "Okay," she said, following her sister into the tasting room, which was where she and Ava ate their meals when they were at the winery. "I guess if you're going to nag me like this, I don't really have a choice."

Sarah and Ava got to the tasting room, and Ava got the promised salad out. She also had packed a lunch for herself, made up of a fruit salad with goat cheese, strawberries, raspberries, blueberries and a honey-raspberry vinaigrette topped with some grilled chicken. Ava's fruit salad was so quintessentially Californian – that was what Sarah associated with the Golden State, fruit salads with goat cheese and chicken, like what Ava was eating. Just like people associate clam chowder with Boston, lobster with Maine, crabs with Maryland, barbecue with Kansas City, etc., Sarah associated Ava's salad with California.

"Now," Ava said as she dug into her salad and Sarah picked around through her own. "Are you going to finally tell me exactly why you're so weird these days?"

Sarah hadn't told Ava what Kevin said to her. It took a lot out of her to tell Quinn all about it, so she just didn't want to repeat the story to her sister. "I'm sure you know about it. I'm sure Quinn told you."

"Yes, Quinn told me a little bit about your meeting with Kevin. But I'm trying to figure out why you're taking it so hard. You don't know anything yet. Your case hasn't been assigned to a judge yet, yet you mope around as if you've already lost Julia. You're not the Sarah I know. I don't see the fighting spirit I thought I'd see in this situation."

Sarah took a deep breath, and closed her eyes. She really wanted a glass of wine to drink with her lunch, but Ava and Sarah agreed that they would not drink at the winery because it was too dangerous to drive home. It was dangerous to drink and drive, period, but it was really dangerous to drink and drive through treacherous mountain roads.

"Ava, you were an attorney. You know the legal system better than anybody. You know how unfair and capricious it can be. You have to understand, this whole thing is on a knife's edge. So yes, I'm human. I'm very stressed about the prospect of losing Julia. And when I'm stressed, I lose sleep and appetite. Please just give me my space. That's all I ask."

Ava put her hand on Sarah's hand. "I'm sorry, I probably came at you a little aggressively. It's just that I'm very worried about you. You're right, I know the legal system, and I know how frustrating it can be to feel that you really don't have control. But Sarah, all isn't lost yet. I think you should probably talk to Kevin before you start to catastrophizing about this."

Sarah nodded. "You really think I'm catastrophizing? You really think I'm just assuming the worst?" Sarah blinked. "You do understand that Julia's life hangs in the balance? Do you know how many times I've walked by the piano room and heard her sobbing in there in the early morning hours before she thinks anybody is awake?"

It turned out that Julia also had trouble sleeping, and, because she shared a room with Emerson, when she had trouble sleeping, she would go into the piano room and shut the French Doors that separated the room from the house, and would sob. Sarah never told Julia that she heard her crying in the piano room, and Julia never knew that anybody was awake when she was in there, so Julia never knew that Sarah heard her.

But every time Sarah heard Julia crying, her heart was ripped out. She wanted to go into piano room and comfort her step-daughter, and tell her everything was going to be okay, but she didn't know if everything was going to be okay so she didn't want to say it. And she didn't really have words for Julia, so that was another reason why Sarah just let Julia cry alone. Besides, Julia probably wanted to be alone during those times.

" I know," Ava said. "This is hard for Julia, and for you, and for Emerson. It's going to be hard for me and Hallie, too, because we care so much about you and Julia and Emerson. It's also going to be very hard on Quinn because she also cares very much about you and Julia, and she's going to have to deal with the fallout when it comes to Emerson. Because you know Emerson will really fall apart if Julia moves away. We're a village, Sarah. That means that we're all in it together to help each other. What I'm trying to say is that you're not alone in this situation, and you need to reach out to the people who care about you."

Sarah dug through her salad as she thought about what Ava was saying about all of them being a village unto themselves. She knew it was right that her friends were there to help her through her situation. It was difficult for her to reach out, though, because for so many years nobody was there for her. For all those years she was with Nolan, she didn't have people who cared about her, who loved her, who would do anything for her. The people who she thought were her friends turned out to not be her friends at all, because they weren't there for her when she needed them. So, she learned to internalize her stress and anxiety, knowing that if she tried to express her feelings, nobody would be there to give her a lifeline.

Now, she had several lifelines – Quinn, Hallie, Ava, even Mary, who was going through the exact same stress that Sarah was. Because, after all, if the worst happened and Julia went to live with Hannah, Mary would be just as devastated as Sarah. Maybe even more so, because Julia was her niece and Mary had loved her all Julia's life. Julia and Mary were so close that Sarah knew Mary would go through her own profound grieving process if Hannah got her claws into her niece.

"You're right," Sarah said reluctantly. "I know what you're saying. I need to realize that my friends and family want nothing but the best for me."

"Right," Ava said. "And don't forget, I was a lawyer. I was never a domestic lawyer, but I can probably help you. I know that you've hired Kevin as your attorney, and he's obviously going to be the person you're going to rely on. He's not going to always be around to answer all your questions. He's going to be busy with other clients, going to court, taking depositions, and everything else that comes along with being an attorney of his caliber. So, when he's not available to answer your questions, I can probably find out a few things. I do have access to the legal database still that has all the case law, so if you ever have a question that's related to your case, I can help you with it."

Sarah nodded. "I definitely will take you up on that. If only the legal database could magically make Hannah not pursue this terrible custody case. If only the legal database could magically assign me a reasonable judge who will look at the facts on the ground and make their decision on that, not on the fact that Hannah happens to share the same bloodline with Julia."

Sarah felt tears come to her eyes, and her sister put her arm around her. "Sarah, I wish that life is fair. It's not. And you're right, it would be nice if we could just wave a magic wand and make things go your way in this case. But I know that you know that there's a pretty good chance that you're not going to get the right judge in this case. That's just reality. All you can do is work with what you have, fight this tooth and nail, and try to get Hannah to see the light. Somehow, someway, you have to make Hannah see that she's

THE BEACHFRONT CHRISTMAS...

going to ruin a young life if she succeeds in this. And that's all you really have in your quiver."

Sarah rolled her eyes. "Ava, if you ever talked to Mary about Hannah, you'll understand that it sounds like the woman will never be talked out of what she's doing. She's very tunnel-visioned. It sounds like she's narcissistic, and if there's one thing I know about narcissists, they will never see anybody else's views but their own. That's the very definition of a narcissist, somebody who thinks that only their view of the world is the correct one. So, you tell me how I'm supposed to talk to some-body who's damaged mentally and make her see reality. You tell me that, and get back with me when you have the answer."

Ava apparently didn't have an answer for that. She knew Sarah was correct. It was obvious by the look on her face. Ava knew, as Sarah also did, that there were people who lived in their own reality. Nothing would ever puncture their bubble. Hannah definitely was somebody who was in that category - at least she sounded like she was by the way Mary described her.

Ava shook her head and continued to eat her fruit salad. "That's too bad. I know what you're talking about, because most of my clients when I worked at the tax law firm were narcissistic people. The whole world always revolved around them, which was the reason why they didn't feel they had a need to pay taxes. When you don't care anything about your fellow man, then you will do anything at all to benefit your-self. I don't know this woman, this Hannah, and you don't know her very well. But I would imagine her sister knows her quite well, and if she described her as a narcissist, then I don't know what to say to you. A woman like that probably wouldn't even settle even if that was on the table."

Sarah got up and got a glass of water, and brought a glass of water over Ava as well. "Mind you, Mary never used the term narcissistic or narcissist. So it sounds like Hannah probably doesn't have a formal diagnosis of anything. But if it walks like a duck..."

"Okay. Anyhow, once you find out what judge you get, let me know. As I said, I'll do anything to help you out. So will Quinn and Hallie, but I can give you legal advice."

"Thanks." Sarah finished off her salad. "Well, it looks like I need to go back out to the vineyards and keep on harvesting the grapes."

Sarah and Ava would have to one day find help to harvest the grapes, because this was backbreaking, labor-intensive work. But Sarah wanted that job, because she loved being outside, she loved getting dirty, and, right now, she loved taking the big knife to the grape bunches. It seemed very satisfying to her, the violence she was doing to those grapes.

Sarah put her big straw hat back on her head, picked up her knife, put her gloves back on, and walked back out to the vineyards. The sun was beating down, as it was probably over 100°, but Sarah barely felt the heat. She was so lost in her own thoughts that the world around her just seemed to recede.

*****

A week later, while Sarah was enjoying a much needed glass of wine from their vineyard, with Quinn, the girls and Ava on the deck of the house, Sarah got the news she was dreading.

Kevin called her to say that the judge they drew, Judge Ryan Kindle, was one of the most hard-ass judges in the entire circuit. "I'm so sorry, Sarah, to tell you this," Kevin said. "I think we need to talk about settling."

Sarah bit her bottom lip. "No. You told me that if we draw the wrong judge that you'll just apply for a change of judge."

"That's just it. This *is* the second judge. The last one we were assigned was also an old-school judge who I knew we

didn't have a chance in front of. So I went ahead and immediately filed a motion for change of judge, and Judge Ryan
Kindle was the one we drew. I sent an email when I filed the
original motion to change the judge."

Sarah closed her eyes. She hadn't been monitoring her
emails like she should. And what Kevin was telling her was
bad, very bad. It sounded like it was the worst news possible.

Sarah felt hot tears come to her eyes. Unfortunately, she
was out on the deck with the girls, Ava and Quinn. She
wasn't going to say anything, because everybody was around.
Julia was staring at her, as the young girl seemed to know
that Sarah was talking to Kevin and that the news wasn't
good.

"Don't do anything. Nothing just yet."

"Well, you have a mandatory session with the mediator. I
set that up, and it's scheduled for two weeks from today. I'm
going to get my ducks in a row, but, as I said, I think you
really need to at least think about what you would accept."

Sarah wanted to scream on the phone that there was
nothing that she would accept. Nothing at all, so this mediation would be a waste of time. But she knew it was mandatory, and that the judge wouldn't schedule a trial until they
went through it, so she was just going to have to suck it up.
But she wasn't going to give an inch. Not an inch.

Instead, Sarah just calmly said "I'll think about it."

And then she hung up the phone without even saying
goodbye, which was uncharacteristic for her too. She looked
at everybody who was staring at her. They all had a worried
look on their face.

" Sarah," Ava said. "You look really pale."

"I have to go," Sarah said. "Ava, don't wait up for me."

And then Sarah walked down the wooden steps from the
deck to the beach, and walked along the beach. There were a
lot of people out this evening, for some reason. Lots of dogs

running up and down the beach, people tossing balls around, couples walking hand-in-hand along the shore. Life was just going on for everybody, and it didn't seem fair for Sarah. How could all these people look so peaceful when her own life was turning upside down? And then Sarah started feeling guilty about thinking this way, because her life wasn't the one that was being turned upside down, it was going to be Julia's.

Sarah decided to call the one person who wasn't intimately wrapped up in this entire mess. Hallie.

Quinn was definitely too close to it, because Emerson was her daughter and Julia was Emerson's best friend, so she was very invested in this whole situation. Ava was too close to it because she lived with Sarah and she was her sister. But Hallie might be able to offer her some kind of objective advice. Hallie was the only person Sarah could think of who could look at this whole thing with an eye that wasn't emotional. Maybe Sarah wasn't seeing something. And Hallie was trained to be a life coach, and one of the things life coaches do is help people with obstacles. And this was definitely an obstacle.

"Hey, Sarah," Hallie said when Sarah called her. "How are you?"

"Not good. You free?"

"I sure am. I mean, I'm at the ranch, but I'm not really doing anything. I'm just staying here tonight because we were having a party earlier, and I didn't want to drive home in the dark. But you're welcome to come up here to meet with me if you want."

Hallie was working at a wellness ranch high in the Santa Monica Mountains. Hallie had come over several times to their house, and Ava always had to include her, because, with Sarah, Quinn, and Ava all living together in the same home, Ava had to make sure that Hallie didn't feel excluded. So

Hallie knew something about the whole Julia situation, but she didn't know a lot.

"Yes, I need to talk to you. I'll be up there, probably within the hour."

And so Sarah got into her car and drove to the mountains. It was getting dark, but she didn't care. Let those jerks tailgate her. She was going to go at her own pace, and no faster.

She didn't really know what she was going to say to Hallie when she got there. She only hoped that Hallie could give her some sound advice.

CHAPTER 15

QUINN

Sarah left, and Quinn didn't know where she went.
Ava didn't either, but Ava just shook her head when
Quinn was going to inquire about what happened to Sarah.
"She's my sister, and I know how she deals with things," Ava
said. "It's best just to let her alone and let her stew."

Quinn took a deep breath. "I just worry. I mean the way
she looked when she was talking on the phone. I saw the
color just drain from her face."

"I know, I know," Ava said. "I saw the same thing. I think I
know why. I think she probably was talking to Kevin."

Quinn looked over at Julia and Emerson, who were trying
hard not to pay attention to what the adults were talking
about, but it was clear they were very interested. Quinn
didn't want to involve the girls in the conversation. She was
still trying to protect Emerson and Julia from reality. Maybe
that was the wrong thing to do, but Quinn didn't want to talk
to them until she knew more.

So, she got up and cleared the table, and motioned for
Ava to follow her into the kitchen. "Julia, Emerson, why don't

you go ahead and head down to the beach with the dogs? We'll do the dishes for you guys."

Emerson didn't need to be told more. She hated doing the dishes, and she loved to play with the dogs on the beach. So, Emerson and Julia walked down to the beach with the dogs and their toys, and Quinn saw them throw the toys into the ocean and the dogs eagerly running into the ocean and bringing the toys back.

Oh, to be free and without care like Kona and Bella, Quinn thought ruefully. Those two dogs were so joyful, running after the balls in the ocean and bringing them back, over and over.

So, Quinn and Ava went into the house and proceeded to do the dishes. "Now, you were saying something about Sarah talking to Kevin," Quinn said.

"Yes. It was obvious she was talking to him." And then Ava took a deep breath. "And I think I know why. I told Sarah that I'd be there for her to bounce ideas off of, and also I'd be there for her for legal advice. So, I've been doing my own monitoring of this entire case. I'm gone over to the court-house a couple of times, to see what pleadings and motions have been filed. And I saw there was a motion for change of judge filed last week. I saw the judge that was originally assigned to this case. His name is Judge Charles Anderson. And then I reviewed all of his rulings in custody cases, specifically in cases like Julia's where the parents are deceased, and there was a family friend who was trying to get custody and a family member who also was, and this guy Charles Anderson ruled for the family member every single time. And he's been on the bench for 40 years."

"Well, that doesn't sound promising," Quinn said.

"No. It's not. So I was relieved that there was a motion for change of judge filed. I was hoping that a new judge would be assigned, and maybe the new judge would be more open-minded."

Ava was shaking as she scrubbed a cast-iron skillet. Quinn saw the body language that her friend was displaying, and it wasn't good.

" Okay, so-"

"So, I went to the courthouse today. And a new judge was assigned. His name is Judge Ryan Kindle. And I looked through his rulings, and he's even worse. He literally awarded custody to a family member over a close family friend, even though the family member had been in prison for child molestation."

"Oh my hell," Quinn said. That, for her, counted as a very strong expletive, because usually she would just say oh my heck. "Really? How is he still on the bench?"

Ava had a dish brush in her hand, and she tossed it into the sink basin. It landed with a thud. " Quinn, if you only knew how many crappy judges there are on the bench, you'd be shocked. Unfortunately, once a judge is on the bench, it's very hard to get him or her off of that bench. Pretty much, unless the judge is committing major crimes behind the scenes, they're untouchable. I know, it doesn't seem fair, it doesn't seem right, but it is what it is. Every profession has its share of morons, and the judicial system is no different."

"So this Kindle guy, he's our guy? There's nothing we can do?"

"No, I don't think there is," Ava said. "Kevin would have to prove this judge is biased or prejudiced against Sarah if he wanted out of his courtroom. Obviously, that would be impossible to prove, because Sarah doesn't even know this Judge Kindle. Anyhow, if it was easy to get out of his courtroom, I'd imagine almost everybody would be trying to get out of it. He seems to be the worst of the worst, and Sarah has the misfortune of drawing him."

Quinn could feel her blood pressure going up. It sounded dire. To say the very least.

Emerson was going to go ballistic. Quinn had some kind of hope on the horizon that maybe, just maybe, this whole thing would just blow over. Sarah would win her custody case, and that would be that. She didn't know why she didn't see this outcome coming, if this was the outcome. But it seemed like it would be.

"So, what happens next?"

"Well, Sarah and Hannah have to go through mediation," Ava said. "Basically that's sitting down in front of a neutral third-party to see if they can settle or at least come to some kind of common ground. That's a requirement. I don't see much hope with that, but I'm going to have to talk to Sarah and see if I can get her to understand the reality of the situa-tion. I don't think she's going to be able to, because she's so emotionally involved. I'm very worried about her."

Quinn started to wring her hands. "I invited Mia, my friend, who is also mentoring the girls with their songwrit-ing, over for tomorrow evening. I wonder if I should cancel that."

Quinn was thinking of Julia's initial reaction when Quinn told the girls that she found a songwriting mentor for them. Julia was devastated, because, as Emerson said, it meant she had one more thing to lose if she had to go live in New York. Would it just be rubbing salt in the wound by continuing to bring Mia around?

At the same time, she was feeling selfish because she really wanted to keep spending time with Mia. She hadn't yet confided to any of her friends the possibility that she had romantic feelings towards her old friend. But, she decided to go ahead and tell Ava. After all, Ava was her best friend, and she would be supportive and would be able to give her good advice on the situation.

" No, I don't think you should cancel it," Ava said. "I know why you want to - you don't want to give Julia false hope and give her something to miss. One more thing to miss, at any rate. But I think that a songwriting mentor can carry her through. It can inspire her to continue with her songwriting endeavors even when she goes to live with Hannah. I mean if she goes to live with Hannah."

Quinn smiled ruefully. "No, you didn't mean if. You said it right the first time. When. It sounds like this is a foregone conclusion unless a miracle happens."

"Yeah. It does seem pretty hopeless."

"Anyhow, I suppose you're right. I should go ahead and keep the appointment with Mia. Because she really knows what she's talking about, and she's really good with the girls. She's a very good teacher and mentor. It's like she was born to it."

"Sounds like it," Ava said. "And you said Mia works with a lot of big-name singers and groups. So she's successful, and she knows what the people want. So, she can really give Julia and Emerson a lot of good advice."

"Yeah." And then Quinn hesitated. "And, I'll tell you as my best friend that my interest in Mia isn't just professional. And it's not just platonic, either."

Ava smiled. "Quinn Barlowe. As I live and breathe. Do you have a romantic interest?" Then she raised her eyebrows. "Do tell. Does she feel the same way about you?"

"I don't think so," Quinn admitted. "I chickened out when I was going to say something to her. I don't know, Ava, I never thought I'd be attracted to a woman."

Ava just shook her head. "Oh, Quinn, you lie. I mean, everybody has somebody they're attracted to who's a member of the same sex."

"What about you? Have you ever thought about dating a woman?"

Ava shook her head. "No, but that's just because I haven't come across anybody who floats my boat. But that doesn't mean I wouldn't be open to it if, say, Cate Blanchett showed up at my door and wanted to go out."

"Cate Blanchett, huh? Interesting choice."

"Yes, and no," Ava said. "I mean, she's a little bit androgynous, she's very intelligent and she's beautiful. But, I'm assuming Cate Blanchett isn't going to show up at my door, and, besides, I think she's married." And then Ava started to laugh. "Anyhow, that's just silly talk. But, in real life, I haven't met anybody who I'd like to go out with who's a member of the same gender, but that doesn't mean that'll never happen. And, let's face it, sometimes men can be a pain."

Quinn started to relax just a little. It wasn't a big deal. But, somehow, she still didn't know if she could go there. She knew she should just get over it, and just tell Mia how she felt.

"Yeah," Quinn said. "I haven't had very many good experiences with men, to say the very least. I mean, Asher was a really good guy, though. But I wasn't feeling it with him."

Ava took a large spoon she was about ready to put away and pointed it at Quinn. "Quinn, maybe you weren't feeling it with him or with any other guy along the way because you secretly always wanted to date women. And if that's the case, then more power to you. It's like I told my mom, who had a really hard time coming out to Sarah and me – love is love. I say go for it."

"Maybe I will. Then again, your advice is coming from a woman who has a crush on her stepbrother," Quinn teased.

Ava laughed. "Yeah, that's true."

Ava had a mild crush on Elijah, who was her stepbrother. Granted, she didn't know she had a different family until just recently, and Elijah and Ava didn't have any parents in common, so it wouldn't exactly be like the Dollanganger family from the *Flowers in the Attic* book, where the brother and sister, Chris and Cathy, fell in love and ended up getting married over the course of several novels. Still, Ava seemed a bit icked out about the whole situation, even if she admitted to Quinn and everybody that she fantasized about her stepbrother all the time.

Quinn, at first, thought the whole thing was just too weird for words. But she got to know Elijah and saw how he was with Ava, and Quinn changed her mind about it. She thought they were very cute together, and she had since advised Ava that she should go for it. Thus far, Ava hadn't taken Quinn up on her advice, and she and Elijah were just really good friends.

"So, maybe I'll get brave and tell Mia about how I feel about her if you get brave and tell Elijah how you feel about him."

When Ava smiled at her and shook her head, Quinn knew one thing.

Neither woman was going to go for it.

CHAPTER 16

SARAH

S arah arrived at the wellness ranch where Hallie worked. She went into the main house, where there were about five or six people gathered around the couches, talking. Hallie was one of them. She saw Sarah and she smiled.

"Sarah! Come on in and meet everybody. This is Claire, Sophia, Daniel, and Marie. They're all clients here."

Sarah shook everybody's hands, and tried to plaster on a smile. " It's good to meet all of you," she said. "How are you liking the ranch so far?"

"Oh, it's so much fun!" Claire said. "Every day we go for a hike, and then every afternoon we go to either a group therapy session or group exercise, and then at night, we play games or just sit around and talk. Today, we had a birthday for one of the other people who are staying here, and we had a little party, with only healthy food, of course."

"It's only the clients here right now," Hallie said. "The other counselors have gone home, but I'm a chicken and I just don't want to drive home on those mountain roads at night. So, I decided just to stay here."

"You're not a chicken, you're smart. I take it you called Conrad and told him you're not coming home tonight?"

"Yeah, but he's busy at the gallery as usual. I don't think he really cares if I come home or not."

Sarah grimaced. She knew Hallie had a thing for her room-mate, Conrad, but Sarah wasn't sure if Conrad felt the same way about Hallie. Sarah suspected he did, but it was hard to tell with him because he was just kind of a fun-loving Brit who had a hard time showing genuine emotion about anything.

" I'm sure he cares," Sarah said.

Hallie just shrugged. "I guess so. At any rate, you're here for a reason. Do you want to take a walk? The trail is lit up for part of the way, and it leads to a really pretty lake. So a lot of people go hiking at night. At first, when I would take a walk at night, I was paranoid that some serial killer who was hiding in the woods would attack me. Can you imagine that? I'm such a goof sometimes."

"I'd love to take a walk," Sarah said. "I need to blow off some steam. And I really need your objective opinion on something that's very pressing."

So the two women walked out the door, and found the trail and started walking along it. "It's kind of neat up here at night," Hallie said. "You hear the owls hooting, and some-times you can even see them flying through the air. And some of the animals are nocturnal, so they're out at night. But I always bring this spray with me, because sometimes there are reports of coyotes or others around here."

Sarah just nodded. She was still so much in her head, that she barely heard her friend talking about the wildlife they might encounter on the trail. "Coyotes," Sarah said absently. "That's kinda weird."

"I guess," Hallie said. "But you lived in Monterey all those years. Surely, coyotes weren't unheard of there. You know one time, I was visiting a friend of mine who lived in San Diego, La Mesa to be exact, and I saw a very skinny dog just running down the street. It wasn't a dog, it was a coyote! That was strange, but we're encroaching on their territory, so it's to be expected to see one once in awhile."

Sarah just blinked. She was seeing Hallie's mouth moving, but she wasn't hearing the words. "Uh huh."

"And you know Conrad and I are getting married next week," Hallie said. "I hope you can be my bridesmaid."

"Sure, sure," Sarah said.

Hallie made an exasperated sound. "Of course, I probably shouldn't be marrying the guy because he's a serial killer and I found bodies in our basement."

"Uh huh," Sarah said.

Hallie stopped walking.

"Why did you stop?" Sarah asked.

"Because something is really on your mind. You literally haven't heard a word I said."

"I'm so sorry," Sarah said with a sigh. "You're right."

"Of course I'm right. I just told you I'm getting married to a serial killer and I got no reaction from you at all."

Sarah knitted her brows. "Wait. You're marrying a serial killer?"

Hallie rolled her eyes. "Come on," she said. "Let's keep walking. But tell me what's on your mind."

Sarah told her the whole story. About what Kevin told her during their first meeting, and what Kevin had just informed her about the judge she was unfortunate enough to draw for this case.

"Oh my God," Hallie said. "That sounds absolutely terrible. I'm so sorry to hear that. What are you going to do?"

"I don't know. That's why I wanted to talk to you. You, of all my close friends and family have the least emotional investment in this mess. You really don't have a dog in this fight, so I wanted to see what you thought about it."

Hallie bit her bottom lip. "So, you really think this Hannah woman is a narcissist?"

" I do. I really do, at least the way Mary describes her, I think she is."

"Well, here's what I think you should do," Hallie said. "Try to figure out if there's some underlying reason why she's doing this. Because it doesn't make sense to me, just what you're saying. It doesn't sound like the woman has any interest in having a child around. In fact, I wouldn't be surprised if, if she gets custody of Julia, she ships her off to some boarding school because she doesn't want her around. There's something else going on. Something else that maybe nobody has really seen. She has some kind of a motivation that she's keeping hidden. If you can figure that out, then maybe you can talk her out of doing it."

"I agree, none of it makes sense. But I don't really know what motivation she would have for doing this."

"How's her relationship with Mary?" Hallie asked.

"Extremely strained, to say the very least," Hallie said. "Neither sister approves of the other's lifestyle. To Hannah, Mary is just too flighty, too non-serious. To Mary, Hannah is just too rigid, too humorless. It sounds to me like they've had a history of just talking past each other, neither able to see the world through the other's eyes."

"Hmmmmm," Hallie said. "It sounds like there might be something there. Like maybe Hannah is trying to get her attention or something. She thinks that taking away some-thing that's very dear to Mary would be her way of getting that attention from Hannah. Like perhaps nothing else has worked, and this is her trump card."

Sarah nodded. It did seem to make a lot of sense, but what to do about it? If Hannah's motivation for getting custody of Julia was as some kind of payback for a distant wound or, as Hallie said, was Hannah's way of getting Mary to pay attention to something, how would that get resolved? It could possibly be resolved if the two were willing to get some kind of family counseling, but it didn't sound like Hannah would be willing to do that.

Nevertheless, it would be worth a try. She could try to call Mary and ask if she would be willing to ask Hannah to get counseling with her. Maybe the counselor could uncover the unconscious, or maybe conscious, reasons why Hannah would want to hurt Mary so badly.

An owl flew across the sky, startling Sarah. Hallie just grinned and pointed. "See, I told you you'd see an owl. I love it out here."

"I can see why," Sarah said. "It's very peaceful out here. And that house that you were at when I came is beautiful. It seems like a really nice retreat. How are you liking it here? I know you've been really excited about this job. Are you still as excited?"

"More and more each day," Hallie said. "I finally feel like I'm helping people better their lives. It's such a great feeling, it just fills me up. I can't tell you how great it is to talk to people and have them listen to me and hopefully take my advice and put it into action."

They started walking back to the house. It was getting very late, about 11 o'clock, and Sarah was going to drive home that night. Hallie was very nervous about driving mountain roads at night, but Sarah was an old pro at driving mountain roads at anytime of the day or night. After all, she had traveled the world with Nolan, and that included camping out under the stars on the top of very tall mountains, and sometimes driving through treacherous passes after dark. Sarah wasn't nervous about driving home, even if she would never drive home after having drunk wine at her winery.

"You want to stay?" Hallie asked. "We serve a really great breakfast in the morning, and maybe you can come on a hike with the others."

Sarah shook her head. "Thanks for the offer, but I think I really need to sleep in my bed tonight. I have a lot of thinking to do, and I do my best thinking when I'm driving. But, I have to say, you've given me some food for thought. Even if I don't think it's gonna work."

"Well, it's always worth a try. It sounds like the legal avenue is not going to be your best bet in this case, so you have to try another tact. I'll be thinking of you."

The two women hugged, and Sarah got in her SUV and drove down the mountain.

Hallie gave her an idea, which was all she wanted from her friend.

It probably wouldn't work, but she had to try.

Julia's life literally depended on it.

CHAPTER 17

SARAH - TWO WEEKS LATER

*S*arah took a deep breath, as she waited in a conference room for Hannah and her attorney to show up. They were there for the mediation, which was required by the court, but Sarah thought it would be a waste of time.

After she had spoken with Hallie about the situation, Sarah went to Mary to ask if she could talk to Hannah about having some family counseling. Mary told Sarah that she would definitely talk to Hannah, but she didn't think Hannah would agree to it.

"Hannah doesn't like to have her self examined, to say the very least," Mary said. "Our parents used to try to get her to see a psychologist when she was growing up, because they both were worried there was something mentally wrong with her. However, she always refused. And, believe it or not, I've asked her over the years to get family counseling with me. I do want a better relationship with her. Besides Julia, she's my only family. Our parents both are dead. But she's always refused. Now I'm not saying that she won't do it, but I don't think she will."

Mary asked Hannah several times in the past couple of weeks if she would go to family counseling, and Hannah had refused. So, that idea seemed to have come to a dead end.

Which was too bad, because the more Sarah thought about it, the more she saw Hallie's advice as being on the money. It made a lot of sense that the only reason why Hannah would be doing this was because she wanted to punish Mary somehow. Because Hallie was right – it didn't seem that Hannah was exactly eager to have a child under her roof. She was an attorney who worked 60 to 70 hours a week. She made half a million dollars a year, so Sarah thought Hallie was right about another thing - Hannah probably would end up sending Julia away to a boarding school to get her out of her hair.

If that were the case, there would be a silver lining for Julia – she wouldn't be under the same roof as the controlling Hannah. So she could probably freely pursue her songwriting talents. She probably couldn't still do her baking hobby if she lived at a boarding school, however. She was baking a lot, still, and her baking goods came in handy at the winery.

Every day, Sarah brought in the treats Julia had baked. Sometimes she baked brownies, other times she baked more elaborate things like lava cakes and éclairs. She also made a lot of fudge, both dark chocolate and white chocolate and sometimes peanut butter and white chocolate peppermint. It was all delicious and sugar-free, so those desserts were a huge hit with the guests who came in for wine tasting and tours.

Sarah and Ava were finally able to open their doors to guests, and every day there would be 100 or more people who would come to do wine tasting and go through a tour conducted by Sarah, where she would take everybody through the vineyards and explain about the processing and harvesting. And then everybody would go into the tasting room and taste various wines, and grab a bottle or several glasses. Sarah and Ava offered the baked goods to all the guests for free, and they were huge hits. In fact, more and more people were coming to the winery because their friends told them all about the sugar-free low-carb baked goods that were offered. So, it seemed that Julia's hobby was becoming lucrative for Sarah and Ava, because it drew in the crowds.

Since Ava and Sarah were so busy with the winery, Mary was often at the house watching the girls. Sarah spent a lot of time with the girls when she wasn't working, and she was getting more and more attached to Julia. She knew that if Julia was taken away, she'd be devastated. Sarah was looking forward to maybe cutting back on her hours now that the harvesting was almost finished for the season. She'd toiled in the field for weeks before she and Ava opened their doors to the public, and now that the grapes were harvested, she could spend more time with Julia. Besides, Ava was busy trying to find help. Their winery was becoming so popular that they were going to definitely need to hire people to help them.

The mediator arrived, and shortly thereafter, Hannah showed up. Sarah was disappointed that Hannah showed up, because she was secretly hoping, or maybe it wasn't so secret, that Hannah wouldn't show up which would be a black mark against her. She would be held in contempt of a court order, and Sarah thought maybe, just maybe, that would be enough to turn the judge against Hannah. Then again, this judge had such a preference for family members that he placed a child with a sex offender just because that sex offender happened to be the child's uncle. There was a family friend who also wanted that same child, a family friend who wasn't a sex offender. So, Sarah wasn't holding out too much hope that any of this was going to come to a good end for Julia.

The only thing she could do would be to look Hannah in the eye and asked her why she was doing this. Ask her to examine herself and ask herself if she really was the best fit for Julia. So that was what she was going to do, in the presence of the mediator.

The mediator was named Carolyn Benson. She was slim, red-headed, pretty, and quite young – she probably was only about 35. She was a family law attorney who did mediation on the side. Sarah looked into her background, and she was impressed with her credentials. She'd worked for CASA, which is a volunteer position that helped abused children. She had tried many cases in the 10 years since she started practicing, and won many of them. She seemed very compassionate and open-minded, which were definitely two qualities that Sarah was looking for in a mediator.

As usual, Hannah showed up in a pantsuit, even though it was now in the middle of July, and it was very hot. June gloom was over, and although July also was kinda dicey as far as weather went - according to the locals, sometimes July was quite cool, and summer didn't really get going until August. But this was a hot July, and the day was over one hundred degrees. Sarah was dressed in a light cotton short-sleeved shirt, a skirt, no hose, and sandals. Hannah was dressed in a full pantsuit, with a buttoned jacket, lined pants, and pumps. Sarah looked at Hannah and felt that she was going to melt just looking at her.

Carolyn smiled at both Hannah and Sarah. And then she explained what she was doing and her role. "I'm only here as a guide between the parties. I can present possible solutions to any conflicts the parties might have. I am here to listen and give advice. I am not here to advocate for either party. My ultimate role is to draw a parenting plan, so I'm here to help the parties come to an agreement for this plan. I do not make recommendations to the judge, and everything that is said within these four walls will be confidential."

Sarah nodded. She couldn't look at Hannah. If she did, she'd lose it. She thought again about the real housewife who turned over a table in rage. At that moment, she could understand the impulse. What she wouldn't give to be able to stand up and turn over that huge table, just to make a point to Hannah that she was not to be intimidated.

Oh, but that wouldn't look good to the mediator, to say the very least.

Sarah looked at her thumbs which were twiddling over and over. She closed her eyes and tried to make her blood pressure recede. She looked at her FitBit, which she wore all the time, and saw her heart rate was almost 100. She was just going to have to take several deep breaths and go through meditation exercises so that she could calm down. Otherwise, she wasn't going to be very good in this conflict resolution.

"Okay, I'm going to listen to each party," Carolyn said. "I'll start with Hannah, because she's the plaintiff in this case. And then, after I listen to Hannah, I'll listen to Sarah. I do not want the parties to address one another directly. I find that if the parties do talk to one another during the mediation directly that this just becomes a food fight. And I'm here to make sure that doesn't happen."

Hannah started talking. "I brought this case because I'm very concerned about my niece. She's living with a woman she doesn't know, who won't give her the kind of religious training she needs. And she's living very close to my sister Mary, who is, for lack of a better phrase, a flighty airhead.

My sister Mary has a great influence on Julia and I think that Mary's influence would be detrimental, to say the very least."

Sarah wanted so badly to be yell at Hannah. How dare she say that about her own sister? Her sister was pursuing her life's passion. Mary was a very good person. She was charitable, giving, loving, warm, creative, and she really loved her niece.

"Okay," Carolyn said in a soft voice. "We will get to the topic of Julia's Aunt Mary soon enough. But Mary is not the child's guardian at the moment. The child's guardian is Sarah. I would like to know what specific issues you see with Julia staying with Sarah."

Sarah raised an eyebrow. She certainly didn't think that Hannah could lay a glove on her.

"I don't believe that Sarah has the values that would be beneficial for Julia," Hannah said. "I want Julia to be the kind of woman who will stand on her own two feet and be independent. Sarah spent two decades of her life with a very wealthy man, during which she was nothing but a lazy handbag. All she did was sponge off this wealthy man, not doing anything but spend his money. And she was convicted of drug possession with intent to distribute. She is a felon."

Sarah closed her eyes and tried to will herself not to stab this woman in the neck. Oh, she should've brought her pruning shears. She imagined herself plunging the shears is into this woman's jugular and watching the blood spurt out.

How did she not see this one coming? She was pardoned by the governor of California, and she no longer was considered to be a felon, but there was no doubt that felony was going to be used against her somehow someway. And, here it was. As unfair as that attack was, Sarah wasn't sure that she wouldn't do the same in Hannah's shoes. It was definitely her soft spot, and Hannah was going to drive in the knife.

Carolyn looked over at Sarah. "Sarah? What do you say to Hannah's accusations?"

"Well, it is true I pled guilty to a felony drug possession with intent to distribute," Sarah said. "I took the rap for a woman by the name of Lauren. I was driving with her, she had the drugs, she pinned them on me, and I pled guilty because I didn't want to be found guilty at trial and possibly sentenced to prison. Lauren's husband confessed everything in a letter to the governor of California, and I was pardoned by the governor. I am no longer considered to be a felon."

"That's just a technicality," Hannah said to Sarah.

"Ms. Stein, I would like to remind you that you are not to speak directly to Sarah."

"Okay, then," Hannah said to Carolyn. "I'll tell you directly that it's just a technicality that she is not considered to be a felon anymore. Just because she was pardoned doesn't mean anything. People get pardoned all the time, but they do not get pardoned because they did not do the crime. They get pardoned for other reasons. In fact, a pardon is given when people accept responsibility for a crime. Which means that Sarah had to have accepted responsibility for what she did to get that pardon."

That wasn't true. There was case law a long time ago that said that a pardon was an admission of guilt, but there were other cases that said that pardons could be given in the case of actual innocence. Hannah was twisting the legal ramifications of a pardon for her own benefit.

Thankfully, Carolyn knew better. "Actually, a pardon can be given in the case of actual innocence. You're an attorney, I'm sure you know this."

Score one against the hag, Sarah thought. A minor victory, but it felt damned good.

Hannah just smirked and looked away. She was not going

to concede the point to Carolyn. In fact, why should she? She knew she was going to win this case.

Carolyn looked at Sarah. "Okay. So your side of the story is that you are not guilty of possessing the drugs."

"That's not just my side. That's the truth."

But Hannah wasn't finished. "The truth is, Sarah also lost her architectural license after she was caught with drugs. And her boyfriend, Nolan, wrote a letter to the architectural board and told the architectural board that he'd witnessed her dealing drugs to children."

Oh, that lie again. That was harder to explain away, but maybe Carolyn would understand that Nolan did that to keep Sarah under his thumb. Nolan wanted to make sure that Sarah wouldn't stray from him, and the best way to do that was to make sure she lost her architectural license for good. So, he wrote a letter to the architectural board full of lies about her. He apparently didn't think her felony conviction was enough to lose her license, and he wanted to make sure her license was gone.

Carolyn looked at Sarah, and Sarah could tell Carolyn was having a hard time keeping contempt out of her eyes. Which was understandable, because the woman did custody cases for a living. She probably came across quite a few people who were involved in dealing drugs to children, and that probably made her extremely angry when that happened. Which made Carolyn human.

"Sarah, what about that letter?"

"Nolan was a very controlling man," Sarah said. "At that time, I was going to leave him, and he knew it. He hacked into my emails and found out that I was inquiring about jobs in San Francisco and apartments up there. So, he decided that he would make sure that I would lose my license so I couldn't leave him. That's why he lied to the architectural board."

Hannah crossed her arms. "Carolyn, Sarah stayed with that man for the better part of two decades. He wrote that letter to the architectural board after they had been together for about four years. Which means that she stayed with that man for 16 years after he did that to her. So, even if it was a lie that he told architectural board, Sarah showed very bad judgment in allowing him to get away with that."

Damned if she did damned if she didn't. She played right into Hannah's hands. It was obvious that Hannah was ready for anything, and had a come back for everything.

Carolyn nodded and made some notes.

Sarah's mind started to drift. She was looking out the window, wishing she could just jump out it. Damn that Nolan. Damn that Lauren. Sarah was still paying for their sins. And here she thought she left all that behind. The reality was, the past was never going to just stay in the past. It was always going to come up again and again. She felt humiliated and degraded all over again. She felt that acute sense of failure that she felt every day of her life when she lived with Nolan.

Why must she always pay for the sins of others?

"Sarah," Carolyn said. "Hannah makes the point that you stayed with the man for sixteen years after he committed a very heinous act against you. What is your side?"

"I don't really have a side," Sarah said with a resigned tone. "I just gave up, that's all. I'm not proud of that. But I just didn't see a way out in my situation. I had no money of my own, my career was gone, and I was a convicted felon so I didn't think I could even find an apartment to rent to me. So I stayed."

Boy, did that look bad for her. If she was any kind of a woman, she would've found a way out of that situation. She would've found a job at Whole Foods or something, assuming they would hire her with a felony conviction, and

141

some apartment would've taken her in eventually. Maybe. And there was always the possibility of working for Dave's Bread, which was the bread that Sarah was always buying because it she loved it. On the package of the bread, Dave explained that he was convicted of a crime and spent 15 years in prison, so his company hired convicted felons because he wanted to give them a second chance.

Carolyn nodded. "Okay. So, Hannah, what else do you have to say?"

"Nothing. I think that Sarah's past speaks for itself. I don't want` Julia being raised by a woman who was so weak that she would stay with the man who would do that to her, assuming it's true that he lied about her dealing drugs to children. And, of course, if he didn't lie, then that's even worse. Either way, I don't believe that Sarah is a good role model for my niece."

And then Hannah started to talk about her problems with her sister Mary, but Sarah tuned it out. This was not going well at all. In fact, once Kevin got the report from the mediator, he was going to tell her in no uncertain terms that she needed to settle for whatever she could get. And even if the judge wasn't a total hardass who always awarded the child to the blood relation, she probably still would lose this case because of her past. It was completely unfair, because she was a different person. She wasn't that same frightened woman who was beaten down by life and her boyfriend. She had a good life now with friends and a career.

But none of that mattered. What did matter was that Carolyn was now looking at Sarah with very different eyes. In her eyes, Sarah saw that Carolyn was looking at her with contempt. Maybe Carolyn tried to hide it, but Sarah saw how her expression had changed. She was looking at Sarah like Sarah was either a liar and had dealt drugs to children, or was a weakling who stayed with a man who destroyed her life. Either way, it wasn't a good look.

For the next hour or so, Hannah went through her entire history with Mary. This was relevant, because Mary was obviously very involved in Julia's life. She lived close by, she watched Julia whenever Sarah and Quinn were not around, and she was very emotionally close with her niece. So, when Hannah went through Mary's various indiscretions, it was something that Carolyn had to take into account.

Turned out Mary was wilder than Sarah thought, but then again, maybe Sarah should've suspected that Mary had a wild side. After all, she did have pink hair.

"When she was very young she slept around with a lot of guys. Lots of one night stands. And the reason why she had so many one-night stands was because she was always getting blind drunk. And when she gets blind drunk, she gets out of control. She starts screaming at people, calling them names, cussing at the top of her lungs."

Sarah raised an eyebrow. "Ask Hannah when these blind-drunk one-night stand behavior occurred."

"They occurred when she was in college," Hannah said. "I heard stories from her friends, and she told me herself."

"With all due respect, Carolyn, I don't think most people should be held accountable for what they did in college," Sarah said. "Especially when they're currently in their mid-50s. I don't think that's relevant."

Carolyn looked at Hannah. "Does Mary currently have a drinking problem?" she asked her.

"Not that I know of. But, one time, Mary stripped completely naked and a party and danced around."

Sarah did hear that story. "She was 23 at the time, and in very good shape," she said to Carolyn. "She did it on a dare. Nothing happened. She just took off all her clothes and danced around, for only a minute or so."

143

Carolyn nodded her head. "Okay, so it's established that Mary cannot hold her alcohol. What other reasons do you believe that Mary is not a good role model for Julia?" she asked Hannah.

"She doesn't have any ambition," Hannah said pointedly. "She doesn't make much money at all selling her paintings and sculptures. She's very talented. She could definitely make a living with what she's doing, but she won't take the necessary steps to sell them. She has a lazy business ethic." Hannah was on a roll now, and there was no stopping her.

"I don't want her imparting onto Julia that it's okay to be poor," Hannah continued. "Yes, she got very lucky in that she inherited that Malibu house from her husband, who inherited it from his parents, but if it weren't for that, I would be supporting her, or she would be homeless. So, the only reason why she's able to even survive is because she got lucky. Julia can't rely on that same luck, so I don't want her growing up thinking she can."

Carolyn was now busily writing everything Hannah was saying. "And what else do you have to say about your sister?"

"She smokes pot."

"That's legal in California," Sarah said to Carolyn. "And she doesn't smoke pot, she takes medicated gummies. It helps her concentrate, and helps her with her creativity. It also helps her sleep."

"How often does she take these medicated gummies?" Carolyn asked Sarah.

"I'm not sure," Sarah said. "But I can tell you that when she babysits Julia, she doesn't do it beforehand. She doesn't even do it before I take Julia to see her at her house. She only does it when she's alone and there's no possibility that she has to watch Julia. So, what she does in her own time, with a legal substance, isn't my concern, just like it's not my concern that some people in the world have a glass of wine every day with dinner."

Sarah could sympathize with Mary's need to take the sleep gummy. Mary apparently had a chronic problem with insomnia, and the gummy was the one thing that helped her sleep through the night. She told Sarah that before she started taking them, she had trouble either falling asleep or staying asleep. Now, apparently, that problem was better. Who was Sarah to judge? Or Carolyn or Hannah?

Mary was finally finished with her side of the story, and Sarah knew the damage was done. It was going to be very difficult to convince Carolyn that Julia wasn't staying with a bunch of wild hippies with felony convictions and drug problems. Carolyn probably imagined in her head that Julia was in the middle of an den of iniquity, were random men with medicated gummies were traipsing in and out, and Mary was getting naked at random bars before hooking up with new random men, and then telling Julia all about it. That was, of course, when Sarah wasn't trying to sell Julia a dime bag.

It was all so silly. So, Mary had a wild past, and Sarah was trapped in a toxic relationship that she couldn't see her way out of. The point was, they both had put their pasts behind them and were much different people. Surely Carolyn could understand that? Surely Carolyn knew that one's past does not define somebody?

"Okay, let's take a break," Carolyn said. "And when we come back, I'll hear Sarah's side of the story. In fact, let's take our lunch."

Sarah gathered her things, and then took the elevator down to the ground floor and walked out into the sunshine. She called Ava.

"How's it going?" Ava asked as Sarah walked along,

heading for a sushi restaurant down the street. She was dying for a rainbow roll.

"Not good. Not good at all. Hannah threw my felony conviction in my face, and then she threw my relationship with Nolan in my face for good measure. Then she dragged Mary under the bus, and ran over Mary for good measure. Sorry for the mixed metaphors."

"Sounds like she's playing to win," Ava said. "What are you going to do?"

"What can I do?" Sarah said. "I told Kevin I wanted to fight this thing down to the wire, but I don't think it's feasible. Too much is against it. I'm just resigned that if Hannah gives me any kind of visitation whatsoever, I'm going to have to take it. If this thing goes in front of a judge, especially an old-school traditional judge who think that women shouldn't have any kind of a sexual past or, God forbid, chew medicated gummies, it'll be all over. And that's just the judge looking at Mary. Once my past gets into the record, I'll be lucky to be able to see Julia ever again."

"None of that should matter, but of course it does," Ava said. "In a perfect world, a judge would understand that past isn't prologue, and people shouldn't have to pay for their youthful indiscretions for the rest of their lives. But that judge probably won't be that nuanced. As for Mary eating medicated gummies, it's no different than having a glass of wine every day with dinner."

Sarah had to giggle. "That's what I said. I said I wouldn't judge Mary for having a gummy every day any more than I would judge somebody for having a glass of wine with dinner every night. You and I think alike."

"Yeah, but unfortunately, if this judge is really old school, he's not going to approve of that, either," Ava said. "Your judge is older, and he came of age and was on the bench when people were getting busted for marijuana and serving years in prison for dealing it. He probably put quite a few people in prison for dealing marijuana. So, even though it's legal as rain now, your judge remembers when it wasn't."

Sarah drew a breath. None of this was looking good. "Anyhow, we're on lunch right now. So, I'm going to go and grab some sushi. I don't think I could eat anything heavier than that. So, I'll talk to you later. I just wanted to call you and catch you up on what's going on."

"Good luck. We all love you. We're all on your side. And we're going to get through it, come hell or high water."

"Thanks, I love you too."

Sarah went into the sushi joint, and went right up to the counter. She ordered a rainbow roll and then got her phone out to look at it while she waited for the roll to appear. She had to take her mind off of this rather terrible mediation session. She knew that by the end of it, the mediator was going to try to draw up a parenting agreement. Of course, Sarah didn't have to accept the mediator's parenting agreement. But she no longer was so confident that she could win. When this entire thing began, Sarah really believed that it wouldn't go this far. That maybe Hannah would back down eventually. Maybe she was trying to make a point and she'd withdraw her custody suit.

Now, there she was, facing a mediator, with the prospect of a judge who wasn't going to listen to the facts on the ground, and having her past indiscretions thrown up in her face. If only she had some kind of solid evidence against Hannah, that maybe Hannah didn't exactly live a pristine life herself. Not that that was going to be dispositive, but it could help.

But, no. She talked to Mary about Hannah at length, and Mary didn't tell her anything about Hannah that would help.

Then again, maybe it was good. Maybe Sarah should never have had any hope in the situation, especially when she found out who her judge was. Sometimes hope is a killing thing. And if she would've found something about Hannah that would be detrimental to Hannah's case, that would've given her hope.

She got her rainbow roll, and ate it. She was so tempted to get some sake with the sushi, but she knew it wouldn't be a good idea to go back to the mediation room drunk. Not that a simple bottle of sake would make her drunk, but sake was very potent and she hadn't been eating much, so there was a possibility she'd feel it. She had to have her wits about her, so she decided that sake wasn't going to be not on the menu for that day.

After she finished her rainbow roll, she trudged back to the conference room. She should've been looking forward to telling her side of the story, and nobody was going be cross-examining her, so it wasn't going to be that bad.

Carolyn and Hannah were already there in the conference room when she arrived. She sat down, and waited for Carolyn to resume the session.

" Okay," Carolyn said to Sarah. "Let's hear your side of the story."

"Sure," Sarah said. "I really want to keep this laser focused on Julia. Yes, I pled guilty to a felony, and it was my fault in a way because I shouldn't have been hanging out with such a shady character as Lauren, the woman who made me take the blame for her drugs. And yes, I was in a toxic relationship for way too long. But I'm a different person now. I'm working at a winery with my sister, I have very good friends and family, I'm doing well financially. But most importantly, I have Julia's interest in mind. And I can tell you that Julia does not want to leave California."

And then, for the next hour, Sarah told Carolyn all about Julia. About how she was a talented song lyricist, how she loved to bake and write poems, how she lived with her best friend, how she had her beloved aunt not too far away. And how she probably would be forever changed if she were forced to live with Hannah.

"She has a whole village here," Sarah said. "We're messy, none of us are perfect, but we love that girl. And we're all working towards making sure she's okay. She just lost her father. She's starting to come out of her profound grief over that, with the help of everybody around her who love her. And I want to know from Hannah what a typical day in the life is going to be for Julia. And I'll tell you what a typical day in the life is for Julia here."

"Hannah?" Carolyn said. "What will a typical day be if she lives with you?"

Hannah cleared her throat. "During the school year, she'll come home around 4:00 PM. And I'll have a nanny waiting for her when she comes home. The nanny will make sure that she will get all of her homework done for the evening. And I plan on sending her to the top school in New York, so she probably will have a lot of homework to do. I anticipate probably around four hours of homework a night."

"Ask Hannah what she expects Julia to study in school," Sarah said to Carolyn.

"Hannah?" Carolyn said.

"I expect her to study all subjects, but at an AP level," Hannah said. "She's going to have a level of rigor that will ensure that she gets into an Ivy League school after she graduates. And I have the money to send her through an Ivy League school. I especially want her to focus on mathematics, science, and any kind of legal class she might be able to take in her high school. I'd like for her to take business classes, public speaking and any course that requires a lot of reading, writing, and research. I expect that she's going to follow me into the legal field."

"Ask Hannah why she wants mathematics and science if she expects Julia to go to law school."

Hannah took a deep breath, and it was clear she didn't like being pressed. "Because to get into a top Ivy League school, you can't just have soft classes like literature, speech and drama, things like that. You need hard classes to impress the school's admissions board. She's already 13 years old. She's way behind in the game. Most kids who are going to go to an Ivy League school are already in prep school, taking AP courses, getting the extracurriculars they need."

"So, what extracurriculars do you expect Julia to engage in?" Carolyn asked.

" I expect her to do an internship with my law firm," Hannah said. "My firm chooses top high school students to intern every summer. I expect her to run for a leadership position at her school. She must join at least one club in her school and run for leadership in that club. It's very important that she has the right extracurriculars on her resume, because if she doesn't, she won't get into Harvard."

Sarah clasped her hands in front of her. Hannah was digging her own grave, but, at the same time, Sarah thought it probably wouldn't make a difference in front of the judge.

"Ask Hannah what about Julia's wishes? What if Julia has no desire to go into law? What if Julia doesn't want to go to Harvard?" Sarah asked.

"Hannah?" Carolyn asked. Her body language and her face were much more positive to Sarah now. She no longer was looking at Sarah with a scowl on her face. Sarah thought that she was on her side now, not Hannah's.

"I don't understand the question. Who doesn't want to go to Harvard? And if she doesn't want to go into law, then I'm not going to pay for her schooling. It's as simple as that."

"Hannah," Carolyn said. "You do understand that Julia is

an individual, and she might not want to go down the path you've set for her. Don't you?"

"She *will* go to Harvard or another Ivy League school, and I suppose I can relent on the law thing as long as she decides to study something else that is lucrative," Hannah said. "If she wants to get an MBA or even a medical degree, I will be fine with paying for her tuition. But nothing else."

"And what if she just wants to do none of those things?" Sarah demanded. "What if she, I don't know, wants to be a grieving kid right now? What if she wants to study poetry in a state school? What if she wants to get a degree in song-writing? What then? Or what if she wants to go to a culinary school because she wants to be a pastry chef?"

Sarah was going against the rules, because she was talking directly to Hannah, but she didn't care. And Carolyn didn't correct her, so it was possible that Carolyn didn't really care either.

Carolyn looked at Hannah expectantly.

"What?" Hannah asked Carolyn. "She spoke to me directly, so I don't have to answer those questions."

"Hannah, what if Julia doesn't want to get an MBA or medical degree or law degree, but she wants to get a degree in songwriting? Or go to a culinary school to become a pastry chef?" Carolyn patiently asked. "Would that be acceptable to you?"

"Of course not. If she does any of that, she's just going to end up like Mary, my sister," Hannah said. "There are two things I want for that girl. Number one, I want her to enter a lucrative field. Number two, I don't want her to have to rely on anybody for income. Not me, and not some loser husband who might leave her in the lurch."

Hannah took a deep breath, and a little vein popped out of her head.

"I know what's best for her, and that's for her to be independent and successful," Hannah continued. "And I'm sorry, but the songwriting field isn't exactly the most stable. And do you know how much a pastry chef makes? About $60,000 a year. In New York City. That won't get her a studio rental in that city. She'll be bringing in around $3,500 after taxes, and studios start at $4,000. Do the math."

Sarah cocked her head. "Okay Carolyn, you now can see what kind of life Julia is going to have with Hannah. Let me tell you about a day in the life that she will have with me."

"Go ahead," Carolyn said with a nod.

"Right now in the summertime, we'll go down to the beach in the morning and try to surf the waves a little bit," Sarah said. "Her best friend Emerson will be with us. And after we take a dip in the ocean or surf the waves, I'll either go to the winery where I work, and Mary will come to watch her, or I'll be around and she'll be hanging out with me. Julia will either do some low-carb baking, which she's excelling at, or she'll write some poetry or songs. Or maybe she'll watch something on Netflix if she wants. Some days, she'll go to the animal shelter and donate her time. Other days, she'll read a novel, because she's a bookworm. Whatever she wants to do is fine with me. Later on in the afternoon, she might have a professional songwriter by the name of Mia come over and help her craft her songwriting."

"Okay, that's a typical day in the summer time," Carolyn said. "What about the school year? What do you anticipate is going to be a typical day during the school year?"

"Well, she'll go to school, and when she's out of school, she can do whatever she wants, as long as she gets her homework done," Sarah said. "I'm not going to try to force her into doing anything she doesn't want to do. I want her to find her own path. I'd imagine she'll continue to write songs and poetry and bake in her spare time once school starts. By the way, her best friend Emerson is an amazing musician. They're a team, Emerson and Julia. They're two peas in a pod, and they're a great songwriting team. A young Bernie Taupin/Elton John combination. Like Bernie Taupin, Julia writes the lyrics. Emerson composes the melody, like Elton John. And, of course, Julia has her faith. I'll make sure she gets to temple on Saturdays and to Shabbat services on Friday evenings. That's very important."

When Sarah mentioned Julia's faith, Hannah snorted. "I'm sorry. I didn't mention faith when I talked about what I expect from Julia. But I'm Orthodox. Which means Julia is going to also be Orthodox. There will be no way that she will be a Reform Jew. No way."

"What do you mean, no way she'll be a Reform Jew? She already is!" Sarah shouted.

Hannah raised an eyebrow. "She won't be when she lives with me."

"Okay," Carolyn said. "Well, ordinarily, I'd put together a parenting agreement that the two parties can agree upon. Unfortunately, in this this case, I don't think that my parenting plan will reflect what I think will happen in court. So, I will refrain. I will ask both parties if they are willing to enter into a written agreement that we could present to the court."

"Yes, I'd be willing to give Sarah two weeks out of the year," Hannah said. "One week over spring break, and one week of the summer break. Other than that, I can't give her any other visitation. Julia will be working for my law firm during the summertime, and over winter break, she will probably be working for the law firm then too. And Hanukkah will be observed during the winter break, so that's another reason why Julia will not be able to see Sarah over that particular break. She will observe Hanukkah in the manner I see fit."

"Oh, two weeks? So generous?" Sarah felt insulted. "Is that all you're willing to do?"

"Yes. Two weeks is plenty of time for Julia to see her Aunt Mary, and if you want to see her, you can see her, too."

Sarah cocked her head. "I have no choice. I'm going to have to take this to court."

"Hannah," Carolyn said. "Are you willing to give Sarah any more time than two weeks a year?"

"No. That's my bottom line."

Sarah felt tears coming to her eyes. It just seemed so lost to her. "Again, I don't think I can possibly allow Julia to live with Hannah. I just see that Hannah will break her spirit," Sarah told Carolyn.

"Well, if Julia lives with Sarah, I see her living in poverty for the rest of her life," Hannah said indignantly. "I won't support her into adulthood, which is what I'll end up doing if she pursues song-writing or becomes a pastry chef. I'll let her live on the street if need be."

"Hannah, it's not all or nothing," Sarah said. "Perhaps Julia will work as a waitress or at Starbucks while she pursues her songwriting career. And becoming a pastry chef has the potential to be a very lucrative career. Same with songwriting. The point of it is, Julia has talent in both of those areas, and these talents should be nurtured, not snuffed out with business and law courses."

"Not going to happen," Hannah said. "Sarah, I agree. I'll see you in court."

At that, Hannah and her tightly wound hair bun and heavy pantsuit got up and left the conference room. She didn't even bother to say "thank you" to Carolyn.

"Thank you, Carolyn, for coming out here and doing this," Sarah said. "I'm so sorry this was a waste of time. But I know it's mandatory, so that's the only reason why we went through with this. I could've told you it would be a waste of time."

Carolyn smiled wryly. "Don't worry, most of these mediations are a waste of time. But, on occasion, the two parties can have a real breakthrough. However, in your case, with a cross-country move involved, it would be very difficult to hammer out an agreement. I wish you good luck."

Later on that day, after Sarah left and called Kevin to tell him the results of the mediation and headed home, Sarah thought about the way Carolyn said she wished her good luck.

Sarah thought Carolyn actually meant it.

Maybe that was a good sign.

CHAPTER 18

QUINN

*Q*uinn had gone back and forth about what she would say to Mia. For the past couple of weeks, Mia had been coming over every day to work with the girls with the songwriting thing. And, every day, when she came over, Quinn and Mia would hang out. Sometimes Sarah and Ava were around, too, along with Hallie. Other times, it was just Quinn and Mia, hanging around like old times. Everybody loved Mia, so she was fitting right in with the group dynamic.

She even brought her dog Rosie over sometimes to play with Bella and Kona. The three dogs got along famously.

In short, Mia was starting to become part of the fabric of Quinn's life. And she found herself getting more and more attached to her friend. Everybody knew how Quinn felt about Mia, and they all were supportive of their possible relationship.

Everybody knew how Quinn felt about Mia except for Mia herself.

There were times when Quinn thought that Mia might feel the same way about Quinn as Quinn felt about her. It was just the way she would laugh, or she the way she would look at Quinn. And Quinn always became tempted to go ahead and tell Mia how she felt.

But, somehow, something stopped her every time. Sometimes she told herself that she didn't say anything to Mia because she didn't want to ruin the friendship. Other times she told herself that she didn't say anything because she was afraid of being rejected. Still other times, she knew that at least part of the reason why she stopped short of saying anything was because the thought of dating a woman was still so foreign to her.

However, one evening, Quinn decided to go ahead and go for it. She made sure that the girls were with Mary in Mary's house, and that Ava and Sarah were at the winery. In other words, she made sure they would be alone.

She felt so nervous waiting for Mia to come over. She never remembered feeling so nervous before, and maybe she never did. After all, Benjamin was the only person, male or female, who had interested her romantically. And she and Benjamin grew up together - they started dating in the 10th grade. So, if Quinn had felt a sense of nervousness before getting together with Benjamin, that sense of nervousness was long past, and Quinn really couldn't remember what that feeling was like.

Did she get butterflies whenever she saw Benjamin back in the day? She supposed she did, but she couldn't remember. At any rate, the butterflies were definitely floating in her stomach as she waited for Mia to come over.

Mia finally showed up, a bottle of wine in her hands. "Hola," she said as she came up the walkway that led to the house. "I brought a bottle of wine because you said you're having pasta, and somehow my usual six pack of beer just didn't seem right."

Quinn laughed. "You're good. Come on in. I have linguini with clam sauce, bread, salad, the works."

Mia followed her into the house, and looked around. "Where is everybody?"

"I sent the girls over to visit Mary. And Ava and Sarah have a function at the winery tonight. They're really doing great with their winery, by the way. They love giving Julia's baked goods away, too."

"How is that custody case going, anyhow? I haven't really asked you about it lately."

"Well, Sarah had their mediation last week," Quinn said. "And it didn't go well, to say the least. So it looks like there's going to be a trial. I think it was just scheduled for November. So it'll be five months of pins and needles for everybody in the house."

Mia shook her head. "What gets into people? I mean, the girl's doing great here. If it ain't broke, don't fix it, you know what I mean? Anyhow, the food smells amazing. I can't wait to dig in, because I love linguine and clam sauce."

Quinn took a deep breath, and tried to calm her racing heart. She got the bread out of the oven, and brought out the salad, and Mia took the food out to the deck. Quinn mixed the pasta with the clam sauce, and put it in a large bowl, and followed Mia out.

"You know what, I have news," Mia said.

"You do? What kind of news?"

"Well, I just sold some songs to an A-Lister. I think I've hit the big time, because this A-Lister is going to release it as their next single."

"Woo hoo! I can just see your song hitting number one."

"Well, you know, I could see your little girls hitting number one one of these days with one of their songs," Mia said. "They're very talented. Mia has a real knack for poetry in her lyrics, and that Emerson, zowie! She's very talented.

You told me she was a prodigy, but oh my God. I'm really happy you're putting her into a performing arts high school, because she can really shine there. Good on you, producing such an amazing kid."

"That's my Emerson. I never knew she could play the piano. I always knew she was a great violinist, but she didn't really start playing the piano until recently."

"Recently, huh?" Mia asked. "You know, when I was her age, I started playing the guitar. And I wasn't very good for a long time. It took a lot of practice for me to get to the point where I was ready to play for people. But Emerson, dude, that girl's ready for the big time. I really hope she and Julia can stay together, because they make quite a team."

"Yeah, she's brilliant in a lot of ways," Quinn said. "It's not always great, because she's so damned brilliant that she could easily outsmart me. And I worry so much about what will happen to her if Julia has to move away. I lie awake at night thinking of that."

"That's rough, Quinn," Mia said. "But you know, if the worst happens, you have a lot of people around you who can help you through. And Emerson, too."

Quinn nodded. "I know. It's just that Emerson's had a hard time making good friends. She's made a lot of friends that she hangs out with, but nobody she's close to. Julia became her first really close friend on Nantucket, and she's her only really close friend here, too. I just worry about what's going to happen when she doesn't have that sounding board. Because you know it's not the same for young teenagers to have adults around as opposed to having people your own age to talk to. You remember 13, don't you?"

Mia started to laugh. "Oh my God yes. Talk about a time in your life when you're embarrassed to be seen with your parents anywhere in public. That was like the worst thing in the entire world, to be out with your mom shopping or something like that, and running into somebody from your school. The first time that happened, I literally ran and hid."

Quinn started laughing, too. "You and I are twins. I did the same damn thing. We're sisters from another mother, I tell you."

"Everybody does that, especially at that age," Mia said. "It's just what you do when you're 13. So, I know what you're saying. If Julia moves away, Emerson will feel like her life is over. She won't want to talk to any of the adults about her feelings. Hopefully she can channel all that frustration into her music, though. That's what I did. Whenever I was sad or frustrated or lonely, I wrote a song. So, just think, if I would've been a happy well-adjusted child instead of the depressed mess I was, I probably would be working in an office somewhere instead of being a professional songwriter."

"You're right. I really hope Emerson can channel her frustrations into something productive if Julia moves away," Quinn said. "But I worry. Somehow, I have a feeling that Emerson might be prone to depression. I haven't seen her depressed, yet, but a lot of times those super intelligent and creative people have a dark side. I worry that Emerson's going to have a really dark side."

"Wish there were words I could say to you to make things better," Mia said. "So, I guess we're going to know all in November. Either things are going to go along just great, or they're really gonna suck for that poor girl. Poor girls, at any rate."

Quinn nodded. "You know, the weird thing is, I don't think I can hate Julia's Aunt Hannah," Quinn said. "I really think she thinks she's doing what's right for Julia. She apparently thinks that if she doesn't force Julia into a lucrative career, Julia's going to end up on skid row or something."

"That's legit, that fear," Mia said. "I can't tell you how long

I thought I'd end up a waitress or a barista or something, because I never imagined I could make a living off my art. A scary, scary time. When I met you, I was living off Ramen Noodles and Van Camp's Pork and Beans. When I was flush, because I had a good night singing on the street, I could buy meat for my Ramen Noodles, but only if it was super marked down as a Manager's Special. Wouldn't want to go back to those days for all the tea in China. So, yeah, I can see Hannah's fears for Julia. Doesn't excuse her actions, though."

Quinn nodded. "At first, I really hated the woman because I felt that she was just trying to control Julia for no reason other than to gratify her own ego," Quinn explained. "But after Sarah told me about the mediation and about what Quinn said about the reason why she wants Julia, I could almost see it. Because, you know, you do have to stand on your own two feet even if you're a woman who wants to be supported by a man. That's the recipe for disaster, being dependent on anybody."

"Not for me, being dependent, but I got lucky that I was able to do what I love and make a living at it," Mia said. "I'm living the dream, man, and I don't take that for granted, let me tell you. And it's a good thing I make a living, because most of the women I date don't have a pot to piss in."

"Or a window to throw it out of," Quinn said with a smile, recognizing a good ol' Southern saying when she heard it.

Mia smiled and laughed. "You know, I never heard that part of that saying about throwing the pot out the window. Why would you throw a pot out the window?"

"Who knows? It's one of those dumb sayings that make no sense, like 'drunk as a hoot owl,' which is something my mom used to always say to me," Quinn said.

"Or sober as a judge. I never knew if that meant that you were sober or drunk when you say that, by the way, because judges aren't always known to be sober."

Quinn laughed. "I think it means that you're completely sober, but I take your point. It probably should mean the opposite."

Quinn brought out the desert, which was one of Julia's patented low-carb chocolate lava cakes.

Mia eagerly dug into the cake. "I still can't get over how well Julia bakes these things. If she opened up her own bakery here in Los Angeles, she'd have lines around the block. Who doesn't want to eat rich and delicious cakes without having to worry about the sugar rush or the extra pounds?"

"Yeah," Quinn said. "I know what you're saying. I have the same questions every time I taste one of her baked goods." Quinn also dug into the cake, savoring the soft chocolate middle that oozed out onto the plate. "Anyhow..." She had a good opening to feel Mia out, because Mia mentioned something about the women she dated not having a pot to piss in. "You talked about dating broke women. You date any broke women lately?"

"No," Mia said. "But you know, I did meet this one woman just the other night. Annika. I met her over at Morgan's. She's just my type. She's artistic, a total bad ass, and she's a lot of fun."

Quinn's heart sank to her shoes. "Annika? That's a nice name. Is she from a different country?"

"Nah. She's from San Francisco. But her mother was a hippy who didn't want to name her kid Andrea or Jennifer or all those generic names women came up with in the late '60s. So, that's the name she came up with. It's a pretty name, which is fitting, because she's a very pretty woman."

Now Quinn's heart sank to subterranean levels. "Are you guys going to go out?"

"Yeah," Mia said. "We have a date to go all retro and go to the Griffith Observatory. She's a big fan of *Rebel Without a*

Cause. And she's lived here for the past five years, but she's never been to the Griffith Observatory. Can you imagine? Especially since she's such a big fan of that movie."

Quinn desperately tried to hold back tears. "What does that movie have to do with the Griffith Observatory?"

Mia gave Quinn a weird look. "You're serious? You've never seen that movie? James Dean. Natalie Wood. Sal Mineo. And Jim Backus, Mr. Howell himself. In a woman's apron. Man, where've you been?"

"I didn't grow up with that movie," Quinn said curtly. She tried to keep the disappointment out of her voice, but she realized it was hard to do so. "My momma never let me watch things like that."

"Well," Mia said. "I know what we're going to do when that movie plays at the Billy Wilder Theater or the American Cinematheque."

"What are those theaters?"

"Theaters that show old movies all the time," Mia said. "I won't let you go another six months without seeing that movie. Talk about a classic. But you know, I've always wondered how James Dean came to embody the height of toughness and cool, because in all his movies, including *Rebel,* he always played a very insecure and angsty teen. Except for in *Giant* - in that movie, he played an insecure and angsty man. He's never played a cool, tough guy like a Steve McQueen-type character."

Quinn suddenly felt out of sorts. She certainly didn't know her old movie stars like Mia seemed to. And, for that matter, it seemed that the infamous Annika also seemed to know old movie stars and old movies. *Well, la di da.* She didn't even know that James Dean had an ultra-cool image. She barely knew who James Dean was, let alone know what kind of persona he had.

"Well, have fun on your date," Quinn said. Then she got

up, cleared the table and Mia followed her back in with her own plates and silverware in her hand. "You know, I have a headache. It just came on out of nowhere. I'm so sorry. But I'm going to leave these dishes and retire early."

Mia looked confused. "Oh, okay. Too bad. I was going to get on your Amazon Prime or HBO Max account and find some old movies for you to watch. It sounds like you need to get acquainted with the Golden Age of Hollywood."

"Sounds like fun. Maybe some other time."

"Definitely," Mia said. "We'll start with some Cary Grant movies, then onto some Bogie, move onto a little Audrey Hepburn, watch a few Marilyns, and end up with some great Steve McQueen movies. That'll give you a rudimentary exposure to some of the actors everybody really needs to know from the old days, along with Jimmy Stewart, Gary Cooper, Elizabeth Taylor and Katherine Hepburn. And Robert Redford. Love, love, love *The Way We Were*. Once we get into the deep cuts, we can watch some Gene Tierney, Myrna Loy, William Powell, Greer Garson and Walter Pidgeon movies."

"Yeah," Quinn said. "Maybe you can invite Annika over and we can all watch some old movies together."

She didn't mean that, of course. She was only trying to be polite.

"Sounds like a plan," Mia said. "Maybe next week we can arrange a date. But you should come over to my loft and watch some old movies on my 60 incher. I've got some comfy leather chairs, lots of popcorn, some snuggly blankets and a big, friendly pit bull who's a total snuggle bug. She'll kiss you to death when you meet her. Fair warning."

Quinn just nodded. "Call me. I'll be there. Anyhow, my head is splitting in two."

"Going," Mia said. "I'll be in touch."

And then Mia kissed Quinn on the forehead, and Quinn sighed.

"See ya," Mia said.

After Mia left, Quinn didn't go to bed. She rented *Rebel Without a Cause* from her Amazon account.

It wasn't half bad.

CHAPTER 19

NOVEMBER - SARAH

$\mathcal{J}$t was the day of the trial, and Sarah was beside herself.

The past few months had been an exercise of triumphs and tragedies. She was a triumphant with her winery. She and Ava managed to create a thriving business, and their wines were on the lips of celebrities around the city, from A-list movie actors and directors, to well-known artists and singers and everybody in between. This was because Kayla's bakery, The Sweet Fantasy Bakery and Catering, got many contracts for celebrity parties for which Sarah and Ava's winery, which they called the Sava Winery, combining their names, supplied the wines.

In addition to supplying the wines for Kayla's bakery and catering company, Sarah and Ava also did a thriving business right there on the winery grounds. Kayla catered many parties at the winery, as the Sava Winery hosted engagement parties, weddings, gender reveals, birthdays, anniversaries and all kinds of other gatherings. Kayla supplied the food and sweets for these soirées, while Julia baked the sugar-free goods. Everybody loved having the option for sugar-free baked goods, because many people were health-conscious. After all, this was Los Angeles.

And, when there wasn't a special event taking place, the Sava winery just did regular business. It always had a steady stream of customers who arrived at the winery to do some wine-tasting, take a tour, and leave home with a bottle or two.

But, even though this should've been such a happy time for Sarah, it was anything but. She met with her attorney almost every week, as they prepared for the day of reckoning, which was upon them. It was time to face the music. Sarah knew she had very little chance of prevailing in this trial, but she didn't want to be defeatist. Julia depended on her to keep her head held high and fight with everything she had. That was exactly what she was planning to do.

She had her witnesses all lined up. Mary, Quinn, Ava, Hallie, Mia and even Emerson were all set to testify about the life Julia had created right there in the Malibu/Venice Beach community. Julia herself would testify, and would be the star witness. Sarah was also going to testify, of course. Mary was also going to testify about why she thought Julia did not belong with Hannah.

Sarah tried not to think it was going to be all for naught. She thought there was an outside chance that all the women taking the stand would sway the judge enough that she could win the case.

Hannah didn't have any witnesses lined up. She was just going to take the stand on her own behalf, and explain to the judge why she wanted custody of Julia.

Of course she didn't have any witnesses, Sarah thought. That was because she probably couldn't round anybody up who would testify that Julia should be with Hannah. To Sarah, the fact that Hannah had no witnesses spoke volumes.

****

Two days later, the trial was over. Everybody testified about how wonderful Julia was doing, how well she was doing in school, how everybody cared for her and helped her every step of the way. Mia testified about how talented Julia was and how much potential she had to become a major songwriter. Emerson testified about their deep friendship and how they always had each other's backs.

Julia testified for half of day two as she told the judge why she wanted to stay in California. She talked about how everybody had helped her overcome her grief for her dad; how she loved Sarah; how it meant so much to her to be close to her Aunt Mary; how she loved her new school; how she never had a friend like Emerson; and how she adored writing songs with Emerson and getting involved with causes with her best friend. She pleaded with the judge to leave her right there with the people she loved and who loved her back. At some point, she burst into tears on the stand as she pleaded some more for the judge not to take her away from her village.

In the end, of course, it didn't matter.

Shortly after Judge Kindle heard all the evidence from Julia's village, and heard no evidence from Hannah - Hannah didn't take the stand, as it turned out, probably because her attorney told her not to because she would just look like the controlling hag she was - Judge Kindle announced his decision.

"I'm just going to go ahead and announce my decision to the parties here in court," he said in a monotone. "I'm going to go ahead and award custody to Hannah Stein, who is the child's blood relation and the only member of the child's family who is willing to assume custody of the minor child. Because it would be disruptive to the child to award visita-tion to the defendant, Sarah Flynn, my order will not include such visitation. I will render a formal judgment to this effect within the week." Then he robotically rapped his gavel on the bench. "It is so ordered."

And then he simply left.

He left behind a devastated posse. Julia was sobbing uncontrollably. Emerson was cussing and flipping off the empty bench. Sarah was sitting at the table, staring at the empty bench, feeling stunned, even though she knew this was coming.

Ava's arm was wrapped around Sarah's shoulders tightly. Sarah couldn't cry, though. She was just too stunned.

She looked over at Julia, who was sobbing on Emerson's shoulder. Emerson was giving the stink-eye to the empty judicial bench.

"I'm going to go back there and talk to that judge," Emerson said. "He can't get away with this. How can he just do this? He doesn't even know Julia. He doesn't know us. How can he do this? Who died and made him God? Who? Who?"

Sarah tried to control her rage. It wasn't just that the judge did this. It was the way he did it. He didn't even pretend that he was considering the evidence. He obviously had his mind made up before anybody even took the stand. And he was so goddamned cold about it, too. He just made his ruling and got up and left.

He completely devastated a young girl's life, and he didn't even have the respect to explain his reasoning. He didn't even stick around to see what kind of devastation he left behind.

Sarah found herself running behind the bench, past the bailiff, who valiantly tried to stop her. Once she got into the suite, she ran through the corridors towards the judicial chamber. She could hear Kevin screaming at her to stop, but no way was she going to. She had to see that judge and give her a piece of her mind.

Out of breath, she got to Judge Kindle's chambers and burst through the door. The bastard was sitting at his desk, eating his dinner, his robe discarded. He was simply dressed in his street clothes. With his bald head, round face and red nose, he looked like any other paunchy, bald, older man who probably drove a Lamborghini because he was trying to impress much younger women, even though he had a long-suffering wife waiting at home.

"Can I help you?" he asked.

The bailiff was right behind Sarah, but, to Sarah's surprise, Judge Kindle waved the bailiff away.

"Yes," Sarah said. "I want you to know what you've done. I want you to go out to the courtroom and see that young girl crying her eyes out. Julia's going to go and live with her Aunt Hannah, and she's going to be a changed girl. She won't fulfill her fondest dreams, and all because of you. How can you be so cold? How can you just do this without any emotion? How can you just rip apart lives without even an explanation?"

"Sit down," Judge Kindle said gently. He paused, as if he was thinking about what he wanted to say. "I'm sorry if I seem like I'm cold," he finally said. "I'm not. In fact, I think I feel too much for the parties in my courtroom. I know that every decision I make ends with a devastated party. In your case, my decision has resulted in a devastated group. These decisions are agony for me. You don't know how they tear me up."

Sarah was now crying. "So why did you do it?"

"The guidelines dictate that if there is a blood relative available to take custody of a child, that blood relative is presumed to be the proper caretaker of the child. I'm sorry, but I didn't see any evidence that Hannah Stein was unfit to take custody of the child. It sounds like young Julia has a loving extended group of close-knit friends and family here in California, and she's very lucky for that. But Hannah Stein is her blood relation. I just have to default to placing the minor child in Ms. Stein's custody in the absence of evidence that Ms. Stein is somehow unfit to care for the child."

Judge Kindle silently offered Sarah a Kleenex, which she gratefully took. She blew her nose and wiped her eyes.

"But you said you won't even award visitation," Sarah said.

"Right," Judge Kindle said. "It would be too disruptive. Maybe after Julia is established with Hannah in New York, the parties can return to this court and modify my custody agreement to include visitation. Until then, though, I believe it's in Julia's best interest to get established with her Aunt Hannah without interference. Let Aunt Hannah get the child acclimated to life with her before disrupting her life to come and visit her Aunt Mary, you and everybody else."

Sarah finally stopped crying. She stared at the judge's desk. "I'm sorry for bothering you," she finally said. "Thank you for answering my questions. You could've thrown me out immediately, but you didn't, so thank you."

She stood up, and the judge also stood up and put his hand on her shoulder. "Again, I'm sorry," he said. "I know your group provided a good environment for Julia. Let me show you out."

At that, Judge Kindle showed Sarah out of the suite of offices. She felt deflated, like a balloon that had all the air let out of it. She looked up and saw her group standing around the courtroom, looking very worried.

All eyes were trained on her as she made her way over to everybody.

She went over to Julia. "I'm so sorry, Julia," Sarah said. "I'm sorry I didn't fight hard enough. I should've been able to do something. I should've been able to prevent this. I'm really so sorry."

Julia was still sobbing, but she stood up and wrapped her arms around Sarah's waist. "Aunt Sarah, don't make me go. Please don't make me go. Please. Please. Please. Please."

"I'm sorry," Sarah said, her voice breaking. "I-" She was going to tell Julia that she was going to go home and get her things packed up and ready. That she was going to have to buy her a plane ticket, and she would go with her to New York to make sure she got moved into Hannah's apartment okay. That she would soon become accustomed to staying with Hannah and everything would soon smooth out.

She was going to say all these words in the bravest tone possible, so that Julia's distress would be minimized.

But she couldn't say any of those words. She just stood there, her arms wrapped around Julia, whose little arms were squeezing tightly around Sarah's waist. It was as if Julia felt that if she didn't let go, Hannah couldn't get her.

Hannah came over. "Sarah, we need to get the logistics worked out," she said. "Maybe you can call me later on and we can get everything worked out. The sooner she can move into my home, the easier it will be."

Sarah just scowled at Hannah. "The easier it will be? The easier it will be? Easier for who? You certainly don't think it's going to be easier for Julia. If you think it's going to be easy for Julia, you just take a look at her right now."

"I'm just saying that there is no use delaying the inevitable. I really want her to be settled into my apartment before the Hanukkah season."

"What about her final exams here?"

"I've already made the arrangements with her new private school for her to take her final exams there. It's not going to be a problem. And it's almost second semester. I already have her all signed up for her AP classes that she'll be taking next semester. Everything is just going to be a smooth transition."

Sarah closed her eyes. The rage she felt at the judge earlier was bubbling back up.

And then, before she could help herself, she punched Hannah right in the eye. That hurt her hand like a crazy. She was surprised how much it hurt her to punch Hannah.

It hurt, yet it felt so good.

CHAPTER 20

DECEMBER - SARAH

*I*t had now been about a month since Julia left to live with Hannah. And now it was Christmas, and Sarah did not feel like celebrating at all. Neither did Emerson.

Although Quinn worried that Emerson would run wild after she lost Julia, that wasn't the case. Instead, Emerson just went dark. That was the only way Sarah could describe the young girl's reaction to losing her best friend in the world – she just went dark. She no longer played the piano, and she barely played her violin even though she was going to the performing arts school and she was required to play her violin every day there. She dressed all in black all the time, and she hardly talked to anybody in the house anymore.

Quinn had desperately tried to get Emerson help, because she recognized the signs of severe depression. And it was obvious that Emerson was suffering from severe depression. Quinn knew that Emerson had lost a lot in her life – she lost her adoptive parents, both at the same time, and now she lost her best friend.

But Emerson refused to go to counseling. "I'm okay,

mom," Emerson would say with an uncharacteristic flat tone to her voice. Emerson was always so fiery. She felt things so deeply. But now, it just seemed that she had retreated into herself. She wasn't Emerson anymore. She was somebody else, almost like a body snatcher had taken her.

The house was just too quiet these days. Sarah would've given anything to hear Emerson and Julia making music together. She so missed that. They really were a team, Emerson and Julia, and now there was only one person from that team and it was sad being around her.

While Emerson was definitely the most affected by Julia's absence, aside from Sarah herself and Mary, everybody acutely felt Julia's absence. Every time Sarah went to the winery and was unable to bring in sugar-free baked goods, she felt it. It wasn't just that everybody was asking about those delicious baked goodies, although that was difficult for Sarah because she wanted to cry every time somebody mentioned them. She also felt it because she felt the absence of everything associated with Julia.

It was crazy. Until recently, Sarah didn't even know who Julia was, because she hadn't met her yet. She was just going along in her life, happy and fine with the trajectory she'd taken. She was okay with the fact that she didn't have kids. She was resigned to not having had children, and that didn't bother her anymore.

But then Julia came in and stole Sarah's heart, and she felt so empty now. It was like there was a hollow core to her, and even the fact that Christmas was around the corner didn't bring her any joy. In fact, if it weren't for the fact that there was a tree up in the corner of the living room, by the fire, Sarah wouldn't even know it was the Christmas season.

Ava tried to tiptoe around Sarah these days. She told Sarah that she didn't need to go into the winery if she didn't want to. Ava had hired a few employees for the winery to be wine tenders, because she wanted to take the burden off Sarah. But Sarah insisted on going into the winery every single day, seven days a week, because she just couldn't stand being at the house. She had to stay busy. She had to have something to fill up the emptiness. She never thought losing somebody would feel this horrible.

During her quiet moments, when she was all alone and she had to live with herself, she wondered if she was so devastated because she had this idea of Julia and her role in Julia's life. She loved Julia very much, but she also loved the idea of her. She thought she finally had the child she could nurture and love, and then she was snatched away. And suddenly, just out of the blue, her life just seemed so meaningless.

" Sarah," Ava said. "Christmas is this Sunday. I always remember how much you loved Christmas growing up."

And that was true. Sarah always adored the season. Growing up, she always watched every single Christmas special that came on the air. During that time, of course, there were three stations on television –CBS, NBC, and ABC. Their television had a knob that clicked when you turned it. So there wasn't necessarily 80 bajillion Christmas specials and movies to watch. There were only the tried-and-true shows that would come on three big networks, and Sarah watched every single one of them when she was young. *Rudolph, Santa Claus is Coming to Town, The Grinch That Stole Christmas,* and, of course, *A Charlie Brown Christmas* were all shows that Sarah would look eagerly forward to every year. She also looked forward to going to the Nutcracker Ballet every year. She also starred in Christmas school plays almost every year.

When Sarah got older, and she had access to the Hallmark Channel, she would spend hours watching those movies on TV. There was one Christmas Eve where she sat and watched the Hallmark Channel from nine in the morning until three o'clock the next morning. That was when she was living with Nolan, and they were having a lot of problems so they were barely speaking, and her friends had abandoned her. So, she spent her Christmas alone, watching one movie after another.

At any rate, Sarah really did love the season. But this year, she just didn't feel like celebrating. "I wish I was celebrating Hanukkah instead of Christmas," Sarah said.

"I know, honey," Ava said gently. "You know, Elijah is going to the temple this Saturday. It's still Hanukkah, so if you want to go with him on Saturday, and celebrate, that's on the table."

"No, I'm good. I was really interested in getting involved in Judaism just because I was raising a Jewish girl. And I hate to say it, but I lost my motivation to learn more about the religion. It's too painful. All of it reminds me too much of Julia."

Sarah was embarrassed to admit to Ava that her interest in Judaism was so superficial. It wasn't that she wasn't attracted to the religion at all, because she was. She loved the charitable, giving nature of the religion. She thought it was a beautiful religion, full of hope and joy and really great music. But she stopped studying Judaism deeply after Julia left. She might pick it back up later, just because Ava was now studying the religion, because she was trying to get closer to her heritage. But it certainly wouldn't be the same to go to the temple without Julia.

Sarah went over to the tree and fingered the garland and the ornaments. She tried to conjure up a sense of sentimentality when she looked at some of the ornaments that she and Ava had grown up with. But there was just nothing. It was if it was any other day. Any other season.

"And, don't forget, Willow and Jackson are going to be here along with everybody else on Christmas Eve."

Willow was now almost 6 months pregnant with a baby girl. She and Jackson weren't married just because Willow didn't want to be, but Jackson was always asking her to be his wife. Jackson was doing very well in his career as an actor, as his first big movie was going to be out within a matter of months. It was a movie that was about the life of Zelda Fitzgerald, and he played Scott Fitzgerald to A-List actor Emma Ross' Zelda Fitzgerald. There was a lot of buzz surrounding the film, and a lot of buzz surrounding Jackson in particular.

Sarah tried to come up with a feeling of joy about seeing the pregnant Willow. Ava was beyond thrilled, over the moon about Jackson having a baby. This would be her second grandchild, and Ava was looking so forward to spending a lot of time with her new grandbaby. And, ordinarily, Sarah would be just as happy as Ava about the impending birth. But she wasn't.

She recognized the signs of clinical depression, and she knew she was going through severe depression. The classic sign was the inability to become happy about anything, and that was what she was experiencing. She knew she needed to get some help, but she was so against taking any kind of prescription drugs for anything. She supposed therapy would help her, but she didn't have the energy to reach out. Even though Ava and everybody in her life was trying to get her to go to therapy, she just resisted.

"That's great, Ava," Sarah said without enthusiasm. "It'll be nice to see them."

*****

That Sunday was Christmas Eve, and Sarah was going to have to put on a happy face for everybody coming over. Everybody was going to be gathering at Ava's house for

Christmas Eve. Sarah and Quinn's house on Venice Beach wasn't quite ready to move into. The renovation was still going on, so Sarah and Quinn had not yet moved out of Ava's house.

Sarah had a problem with the fact that she was living with Quinn, because the original reason why she agreed to live with Quinn was because she needed Quinn to help her raise Julia, and she was going to help Quinn raise Emerson in turn. Now she didn't have Julia to worry about, so she felt like she was going to be useless to the household. She was going to still help Quinn look after Emerson, of course, but there wasn't going to be Julia around anymore so the entire arrangement seemed so sad to her now.

The day was typical weather for December, at least that was what the locals said. It was 40° overnight, 68° during the day, and, since they lived right on the water, it was cooler at Ava's then Sarah expected it would be in Southern California. She lived in Monterey before she moved to Nantucket, but Monterey, being in Northern California, was a lot cooler all year round. No snow, but cool temperatures.

Hallie came over early, along with her roommate, Conrad. Samantha showed up with Grayson. Jackson showed up with Willow. Mary showed up by herself.

When they came over, Sarah managed a small smile and perfunctory hugs, and then she excused herself to go out to the deck to watch the waves come in. She just didn't feel like celebrating with everybody else, and she resented being forced to do so. What she really wanted to do was to get in the car and go to a hole-in-the-wall bar where nobody knew her and have a few beers.

As she sat on the deck, she heard Mia arrive with her girlfriend, Annika. Mia and Annika had been dating for the past few months, and though she knew that Quinn still carried a torch for Mia, Quinn was very game about hanging out with

Mia and Annika. The three of them had weekly classic movie nights over at Mia's loft, because Mia was appropriately shocked that Quinn knew nothing about the old movie stars of the past. Now Quinn was learning about these old movies and stars, and she found that she really loved screwball comedies, film noirs, gangster films and all the *Thin Man* movies starring William Powell and Myrna Loy. She told Sarah she thought those movies were "a hoot."

And she really loved Cary Grant. "They don't make men like that anymore, that's for sure," Quinn had told Sarah.

"No, they don't," Sarah had said, and that was for sure. Cary Grant was a singular talent, a combination of extremely good looks, perfect comic timing, charisma and a certain *je ne sais quoi*. It was a crime that he never won an Oscar. Shocking, really.

Quinn was still sad about the fact that she missed her chance with Mia, but she seemed to accept it. It was painful for her to hang out with them, but, at the same time, she just loved being around Mia so much that she accepted the situation. Mia no longer came around to help Emerson compose music, of course, because Emerson was no longer playing music. She was forced to when she was at school, but at home, she just didn't play at all. So, because Mia didn't come around to coach Emerson, Quinn went to Mia's place more often.

Ava came out. "Sarah, we're about to sing Christmas carols. We're trying to talk Emerson into playing the piano for us, because she's so good, but if she doesn't, it looks like I'm going to be the one who's going to play the piano. Can you imagine?"

No, Sarah couldn't imagine that. Ava hadn't had a piano lesson since she was 12, and she never had the talent to keep going. She was just too frustrated with her inability to progress on the instrument, and that was why she quit. Yet, she was going to be the one who was going to play the piano for everybody. Oh, joy.

"Ava, don't hurt yourself," Sarah said in a teasing voice. "Maybe you guys should just stick to playing CDs and singing along to those. Or, better yet, you should find a Christmas station on Spotify to sing along to."

"Thanks a lot," Ava said. "I'm not that bad."

Sarah just raised an eyebrow and turned her head away, back towards the sea. "You're not that good, either. Don't get me wrong, you're great at all kinds of things, but piano-playing ain't one of them."

"Sisters," Ava said with a laugh. "You can always count on sisters to tell you the truth in the bluntest terms possible."

Sarah tried to laugh along with Ava, but she wasn't feeling it.

"Ava, I hope you don't mind if I beg off tonight. I'm just not in the mood to celebrate."

Ava nodded her head. "I understand. You can go ahead and do what you want."

Sarah stood up because she was going to get her coat and her beanie when the doorbell rang. Quinn went to the door to open it, and then she screamed.

"Sarah, Sarah, Sarah, get in here!" she shouted.

Sarah went into the foyer, and she almost fainted dead away.

There was Julia.

And she had a huge suitcase.

CHAPTER 21

DECEMBER - QUINN

*Q*uinn was really excited about Christmas. She loved everything about the holiday season, because for her, it was a time to give thanks for all she had. And she knew she had a lot.

What she didn't have was a romantic interest. Not that she didn't still have romantic feelings for Mia, because she did. If anything, in the past few months, as Quinn and Mia hung out more and more, her feelings for Mia got stronger. Unfortunately, during that same period of time, it seemed that Mia's feelings for Annika also got a lot stronger.

She tried to tell herself that was fine. Annika was a cool person. She was a Pilates instructor in the Valley, and she grew up in the Bay Area, where her parents were a part of a commune of 11 adults and 10 children who lived in a rambling six-bedroom house in San Francisco. It was a fascinating existence, and Quinn couldn't help but ask a ton of questions about Annika's childhood, because she was so interested in hearing the stories of Annika when she was growing up with her hippie parents.

"It was great," Annika said. "Everybody in the communal

house were musicians and artists and actors and just every kind of creative type. Nobody had any money, which was a reason why so many of us lived in the same house, but there was a lot of fun and frivolity in that house."

So, even though Quinn was profoundly jealous of Annika, because Annika was dating Mia, she also really liked the woman. As much as she wanted to hate her, she just couldn't.

So, she was more than happy to invite both Mia and Annika over for Christmas Eve. They both said they were looking forward to it.

But, when Mia and Annika showed up, Quinn got a most unpleasant surprise. Annika was sporting a huge engagement ring that she showed off to everyone. Mia was all smiles, too, as she told everyone that she and Annika were engaged.

And, all at once, Quinn felt a sinking feeling. There was a part of her that thought that Mia and Annika would break up one day. And she would be there to pick up the pieces, even if she wasn't quite ready to jump into a relationship with Mia. Now, apparently, her chance was slipping away.

What could she do? Everybody was there. Hallie had just arrived with Conrad, and, of course, Ava, Sarah, Samantha, Grayson, Jackson, Willow and Mary were all there in the house, celebrating Christmas. Emerson was around some-where, probably in her room, because that was all she ever did was hang out in her room, not talking to anybody. Even though it was Christmas, Quinn wasn't going to force her to hang out with everybody.

And then, out of the blue, Julia arrived. Quinn's eyes got huge, as she ran to hug the girl along with everybody else. And then she went up to Emerson's room, and excitedly told her to come down to the living room, because Julia was there.

Emerson didn't know why Julia was there, and neither did anybody else. It was possible she was just there because she wanted to spend the holidays with everybody, even though she didn't observe Christmas. Maybe Hannah backed down and let Julia see everybody over the holiday season.

She didn't know, but she did know was that Julia was there.

In a few minutes, so was Hannah.

So, confusion continued to reign.

CHAPTER 22

DECEMBER - MARY

*W*hen Julia arrived on Christmas Eve, Mary was thrilled to see her. But she didn't really know what it meant to see her niece there at the house. Like everybody else, she didn't know what was going on. She didn't know if Julia was there for a day, or a week, or, dare she think...No, she definitely couldn't get her hopes up that her sister changed her mind about caring for Julia.

So, everybody crowded around Julia. Emerson was jumping up and down, Sarah was crying, and everybody else was laughing and crowding the poor girl. Julia came over to Mary.

"Surprise, Aunt Mary!" she said. "I'm back for good!"

Sarah heard the words, and she immediately came over. "Oh my God, you're kidding me. You're here for good? Really?"

Sarah was really crying, and so was Emerson by now. She knew that Quinn was having problems with Emerson lately because she was so severely depressed. But the Emerson that was in that living room right now was definitely not a depressed girl. She was smiling from ear to ear, and she kept hugging Julia.

Mary couldn't believe what was happening. And Hannah was there, so Mary knew she was going to have to talk to Hannah and see what was going on.

"We wanted to surprise everybody, which is why I didn't tell anybody we were coming," Hannah said. "It was Julia's idea just to show up here. She's so dramatic. She just wanted to give everybody a heart attack, I guess. At any rate, mission accomplished."

"Hannah, it's good to see you," Mary said. "But I don't trust you and I don't trust Julia saying she's going to be staying here for good. Why do I think you're using her to get all of her hopes up, and then snatch it away at the last second?"

"You really think very poorly of me, don't you?" Hannah asked.

"Yes. After the stunt you pulled with taking Julia, yes, I'm not giving you the benefit of the doubt."

"Let's go out on the deck," Hannah said.

It was then that Mary noticed that Hannah wasn't looking like she usually did. She didn't have her hair up in a tight bun. Rather, she had her hair softly framing her face in a layered bob that actually was very flattering for her. Instead of her usual pantsuits, which she always wore, she was wearing a pair of jeans and a blue sweater with the words "too lit to quit," and a Menorah stitched on the front. She was wearing a pair of leather boots over her jeans. She was almost unrecognizable, now that Mary thought about it.

Mary and Hannah went out on the deck. It was cold, and it was 4 PM, so the sun was almost completely gone and darkness had almost descended. The Christmas lights that Ava had strung around the deck were lit up, green and red. There was also a Christmas tree out on the deck, and that, too, had just lit up because the lights were solar and they didn't come on until dark.

"Hannah, what's going on?"

Hannah took a deep breath. "I think I came to my senses after I got Julia to my apartment in New York."

"How so?" Mary asked. She was starting to feel hopeful, but she tried to dismiss that feeling of hope because she didn't want to be let down again.

"I was helping her unpack, and I came upon her poems and the songs she wrote," Hannah said. "And I realized she really has a rare talent. But, at first, I didn't want to acknowledge any of that. I was so focused on making Julia go on the path I set for her that I didn't even stop to think about why I wanted her to go on that path."

"Okay," Mary said. "Go on."

"Well, I kept finding her songs and poems, and I started getting angrier and angrier every time I saw them," Hannah said. "I had no idea why I was getting so angry about it. I only knew I was. It was as if those songs were mocking me somehow. I know, it sounds weird, but I felt that way about them."

Mary nodded her head. She wanted her sister to go on. She had a feeling that this just might be the breakthrough she always wanted.

"I finally decided I was going to take Julia's entire trunk of poems and songs and put it in my attic," Hannah said. "Well, it's not really an attic, because I live in a condo, but it's what I call my attic. It's my storage room. And I dragged that trunk into that storage room, and while I was in there, I came across something I hadn't seen a long time. It was my own trunk. It was filled with my paintings I did when I was young. They were amateurish, rudimentary, nothing like yours. I never had your talent."

That was the first time Hannah even acknowledged that Mary had talent. "You think I'm talented?"

"Wildly talented." And then Hannah took a deep breath. "My work was starting to suffer after Julia came to live with me. And I told myself that my work was suffering because I was worried about her and meeting her needs. The partners, they told me I needed to see a therapist. Otherwise, I wasn't going to be able to take on any more clients. I guess some of the clients had complained about a few things I did, I won't go into it, and the partners were worried about being sued. So that's why they told me to see a therapist. They knew it wasn't like me to make a lot of mistakes."

"You saw a therapist?" Oh, that had to have been interesting.

"Yes, I self-examined for the first time in my life. And, you know, because I wanted to return to work right away, I went to a therapist every single day. For three hours a day. I was determined I was going to get to the root of why my work was suffering. And why my suffering work ethic coincided with Julia coming to live with me."

"So, what did you find out about yourself?"

Hannah paused for a long time. She was looking into the distance at the raging ocean, a contemplative look on her face.

"Because I was going to therapy so intensely, and I really wanted to get to the bottom of my issues, I discovered one thing," she finally said after several minutes of watching the ocean silently. "I took Julia because I wanted to punish you."

Hannah went to the edge of the deck and put her arms on the railing. She took a deep breath, in and out. This was obviously painful for her, so Mary just stood back and waited for her to explain what she meant by wanting to punish Mary.

"I hated you," Hannah finally said. "You were doing exactly what I wanted to do, but I never had the talent to do it. I hated you for squandering that talent."

"Um, I don't think I'm squandering my talent," Mary said. "I work every single day."

"But you *are* squandering it," Hannah said. "You're making all these paintings, and nobody's buying them because nobody knows about them. I think you should try to share your artistic gift with the world, but you're not doing anything about that. And I hated you for that, because you got all the talent and you weren't doing anything with it, and I wanted that talent. It just seemed to be such a waste."

"I see. So that's why you told me that I needed to get my old job back in corporate law if I wanted you to drop the custody suit."

"Yes. I wanted you to be as unhappy as I am."

That was a first time Mary heard that Hannah was unhappy. "You're unhappy?"

"Desperately unhappy," Hannah said. "What I wouldn't give to have one-tenth of your talent. It just seems so unfair that God gave you all these artistic gifts, but he gave me all the ambition in the family. I wanted my ambition to go towards my own artistic endeavors. But, you know, I tried to sell my own paintings. I did that a lot in my spare time, putting them on eBay and trying to find galleries who would accept them. I even have my own Etsy store. But I didn't sell a single painting. It was humiliating."

"Well, maybe you admire me, but I really admire you," Mary said. "You're making beaucoup money. You're one of the most respected corporate attorneys in New York City. That ain't nothing."

Hannah smiled. It occurred to Mary that that was the first time she had seen a genuine smile on Hannah's face been a long time. Too long.

"I thank you for saying that," Hannah said. "But, after about 40 hours of therapy over a two-week period, I wore out my shrink. I also came to the conclusion that I can't go on doing what I'm doing. I'm digging myself into an early grave. So, Julia is definitely back for good." She paused. "And I was wondering if I could possibly interest you in a business relationship."

Mary narrowed her eyes. "What kind of a business relationship?"

"Well, I also realized that even though I have no artistic talent of my own, I'm very interested in art. So, I bought a gallery. In the arts district here in Los Angeles, so, of course, I'll be moving to the area. I've been focusing my eye on several different artists I've seen on the Internet. But I'd really like to put your paintings in my art gallery. I have a lot of money saved up. Because, after all, I've been working like a dog since I was 25 in the legal field, and not spending very much money. So, I have a lot of money to put into this endeavor, including into marketing. I'd like you to be my star artist."

Mary blinked. Was this really happening? If she was a believer in Christmas, which she wasn't – after she left the Jewish faith, she really didn't see a need to pick up any other faith - but if she were a believer in Christmas, she'd have to say she was experiencing a Christmas miracle. Her sister might actually become a real sister to her. Finally. While it was great that Hannah was offering to sell Mary's paintings in Hannah's new art gallery, that wasn't the reason why Mary was astounded. She was more astounded by the fact that Hannah apparently, deep down, maybe all along, loved her. What Hannah did with this art gallery thing was an act of sisterly love.

Mary impulsively hugged Hannah, and Hannah hugged Mary right back. " Oh my God, is this happening? Are you really going to treat me like a sister? After all these years?"

Hannah just took a deep breath. "Yes. I am. You see, I think I've hated you all these years because you had what I wanted. And now, I think I've come to terms with that. And I'm ready to help you achieve your potential. I can think of no better way to spend my millions than to help you and every other starving-yet-talented artist get some exposure." And then she paused for a long time. "I'm sorry, Mary. I'm really sorry for putting everybody through this Julia mess. I used that poor girl, because I knew it would hurt you if I took her away. That's how twisted I was. And I'm just so glad I was able to figure that out before it was too late."

Mary realized that Ava's friend Hallie was right on the money when she told Sarah that she thought Hannah had an ulterior motive for taking Julia. That Hannah wanted to punish Mary for something. Hallie really had an intuitive gift.

Mary hugged Hannah again, and, she decided that maybe she did believe in Christmas.

Because if this was not a Christmas miracle, she didn't know what was.

CHAPTER 23

SARAH

*W*hile Mary and Hannah were out on the deck, Sarah was hugging Julia so tight she was surprised Julia didn't suffocate. Emerson eagerly tapped Sarah on the shoulder.

"Dude, she can't breathe," she said.

So Sarah reluctantly let go of Julia, and Emerson wrapped her own arms around Julia and squeezed her so tight that Sarah was surprised Julia didn't suffocate.

" Are you really back for good?" Emerson asked her.

"Yes, I'm really back for good. Can you believe it? It turns out my Aunt Hannah was human after all. I always thought she was some kind of an evil cyborg or something like that. But she's human. And I really like her. At least, I like her now. I hated her about a month ago."

"What happened?" Emerson asked.

"She just changed her mind. About everything. I was going to email you and let you know we were coming, but then I thought it would be so much more exciting to just show up here and see everybody's reaction. I'm sorry I didn't email you and tell you."

"It's okay. Listen, now that you're here, I say we go over to the piano and we rock this house down this Christmas. Let's play some of the songs we've been getting ready."

Emerson cracked her knuckles, and dragged Julia by the hand over to the piano. Everybody gathered around to listen to the two young girls. They were amazing, as Julia sang song after song for two hours. That was how much material they'd written together.

After they entertained the group with their original songs, Emerson said "Let's do some standards. It is Christmas, and what a great Christmas it is. I don't think I could've asked for a better Christmas present."

"I don't think I can ask for a better Hanukkah present," Julia said.

Sarah thought that she couldn't ask for a better Christmas or Hanukkah present, either.

Julia was back. All was right with the world.

CHAPTER 24

QUINN

*Q*uinn was so happy to see Julia. Everybody was thrilled to see her, but Quinn knew that this was a lifeline for Emerson. She was so worried about Emerson. She saw her young daughter slipping away from her, and she didn't know what to do. Now, Julia was back, and so was Emerson.

And if it weren't for the fact that Mia was engaged to Annika, Quinn would have to say this was the best Christmas ever. Mary and Hannah had made up and mended fences. Julia was back. Emerson was playing the piano again with a huge smile on her face. What more could she ask for?

She drank a lot of champagne that day. Probably a bit too much, considering she didn't really eat that day because she forgot to. And, when everybody had left, she went out to her deck. It was around 11 o'clock, and everybody had gone to sleep.

Then she heard Mia's voice. "I'm so sorry Quinn. I left my laptop computer." Mia had brought her laptop over that day, because she was still hopeful she could interest Emerson in doing a little bit of song writing for Christmas. At first, of course, Emerson had no interest. But, after Julia showed up, Emerson was very interested and wanted to see what Mia had come up with. So, after Emerson and Julia had entertained everybody with their singing, Emerson, Julia, and Mia did a little impromptu songwriting. Within 1/2 hour, the three had come up with a Christmas song for everybody, and they performed it live to everybody's delight.

"Oh," Quinn said. "I see you have that laptop in your hands. So I guess I'll be seeing you soon."

"You will." And then Mia hesitated. "You okay? You seem a little off."

Quinn nodded. "I'm so happy for you and Annika."

"Yeah," Mia said. "I got a little spontaneous."

Quinn just smiled.

Mia got very quiet for a long time. Quinn had no idea what was on her mind, but she didn't press. She seemed to sense that she needed to give Mia space to say something important.

"Quinn," Mia finally said. "Annika thinks I might be in love with you."

Quinn turned to Mia. "She does? Why does she think that?"

"Women's intuition. I told her that it was a fine time to be telling me now that she thought that. But she wanted me to tell you. Do you think that's crazy?"

"No." Quinn said. And then she paused for a long, long time. "Because I feel the same way about you," she finally admitted.

There. She said it. That wasn't so hard, but maybe it was the champagne talking.

"You do? For how long?" Mia asked.

"Oh, probably for 30 years. Even though I never acknowledged it. I think that's why I never reached out to you over the years. I was afraid of my feelings."

Mia shook her head. "Quinn, do you know I've carried a torch for you all these years too? Man, I never thought you would've felt the same way about me. I never thought you'd date a woman. But, you know, I guess I should've asked you all those years ago. Maybe we could've been together all this time like an old married couple. We'd be bickering right now about who used the rest of the toilet paper without replacing the roll."

Quinn laughed. " I don't know what I would've said back then even if you would've told me about your feelings. I was married to Benjamin, and my feelings confused me then and they're confusing me now. But, I guess it's too late to do anything about it."

"No, never too late," Mia said. "I think Annika understands. She accepted my ring, but she was the one who told me I needed to get my feelings for you sorted out before we went forward. And, I guess that's what I'm doing right now. Sorting out my feelings."

Quinn felt the butterflies. "But you said you wanted to set me up with a woman. I don't understand."

"I only said that because I was embarrassed about asking you if you would date a woman. I didn't want you to think I was asking for myself, which I obviously was."

Quinn laughed. "So, what does this mean?"

"It means I have to break it off with Annika. Because I don't want to go another day not being with you."

And then Mia kissed Quinn. Quinn felt it to her toes.

That was how Quinn knew that it was right with Mia. Not that Quinn would put a label on herself. But she realized that Mia was probably right about one thing. Well, Mia was right about a lot of things, but something she said stuck out with Quinn and explained her confusion.

You really do fall in love with the person, not the gender.

And Quinn was in love with Mia.

It really was the best Christmas ever.

I HOPE you've enjoyed this series so far! There's more to come - much more! So, to find out about new books coming out, sign up for my mailing list!

Sign   Up:https://mailchi.mp/1e4784c41707/ainsley-keaton-mailing-sign-up

A new book in the series will probably be published in January, so make sure you sign up so you can find out all about it! Thanks again for reading!

Made in the USA
Monee, IL
26 September 2024

66569496R00115